CLOSE YOUR EYES AND SEE

Second Edition: December 2023

10 9 8 7 6 5 4 3 2

Vecteezy.com

Novels By Bernard Cenney:

SPARROW'S TEARS

CLOSE YOUR EYES AND SEE

TIMELESS TERROR

TIMELESS SOLDIER

TIMELESS EMBRACE

TIMELESS DESTINY

CLOSE YOUR EYES AND SEE

BERNARD CENNEY

AUTHOR'S NOTE:

This literary manuscript is entirely a work of fiction. Any similarity or resemblance to businesses, organizations, places, names, characters, real persons, incidents, or events is purely coincidental, unintentional, imaginary, or used in a fictitious manner.

In Memoriam:

JAMES B. CENNEY
19 OCT 1989 — 11 OCT 2004

LOVED FOREVER

Send your tax deductible contributions to find a cure for children's hypertrophic cardiomyopathy to:

www.childrenscardiomyopathy.org

Thank you.
Bernard Cenney

DEDICATION:

Special thanks go to my wife, Kongsri Cenney.
Over thirty-seven years ago in Southeast Asia, Kongsri left her family, her country, and everything that was familiar to her in order to marry a young American Special Forces Captain. She took my hand and never looked back. We have supported each other in conflict and peace, hardship and success, sorrow and joy. Through it all she has loved me unconditionally and never left my side.

Bernard Cenney
Lt. Colonel (Retired)
United States Army
8 January 2024

PREFACE

Perhaps someone who is mourning will find solace in the following.

The worst experience to suffer is the death of your child.

The hypertrophic cardiomyopathy death of my fourteen-year-old son, James Cenney, was a tragedy that nothing in this present world can ever make right. James was young, innocent, and just starting life. One day he was playing his guitar; the next day he was not. One day he was playing football and exercising; the next day he was not. One day he was going to school, laughing, and joking; the next day he was not. One day he was here — the next day he was gone. No father should outlive his child.

James' unexpected death shattered my wife, my daughters, and me. Parents who lose their child never bounce back. Speaking for myself, his death eroded my spirit, my resiliency, my resolve, my fortitude, my joy, my hope, and my self-worth. It became impossible to feel any sort of happiness for years.

The sheer madness and incomprehensible horror of his death destroyed my understanding of a loving God. Suffering became a daily companion. I convulsed at the clichés of "all things happen for a reason," or "God never gives us any burden we can't handle." I avoided those who declared they were "blessed by God." It made me feel as if my life was surely cursed by him.

I had seen death before, privately and in my military career. But this was intensely more personal, more visceral, more agonizing. Surely God did not want this to happen; surely God was mourning just as we were; surely God was in despair over this tragedy; surely God — as my father — empathized.

I started to have vivid dreams and visions of James. I documented and kept a record of them all. I could never (and still can't) control the mental image of my son James passing away. I have always (and still do) blame myself for not being able to somehow save him. It became an unimaginable situation. It began replaying itself, over and over, every day of my life. I was in a very dark place.

The military community at Fort Sam Houston provided us with overwhelming support. Group and individual therapy was helpful at first, but soon was not enough for me. Depression developed into apathy to even want to wake up. A terrible schism evolved between wishing for nonexistence, and a father's obligations to the rest of his family.

I just couldn't believe that James had passed away. Sometimes I think he will walk through the door, and everything will be as it once was. After he died, I thought the world would end. In my mind, I waited for the end to come. But it didn't. People went to work, children went to school, and life kept grinding on. My mind tore to pieces over whether to stop moving or to keep pushing onward.

My wife and daughters were suffering terribly as well, perhaps even more than me. Together as a family, we comforted and supported each other. I don't believe it would have been possible for me to move on without the love of my family. I felt that I had to show strength for them. I had to be the father to push everyone onward and hold the family together. If I gave up, I would have failed everyone. I knew that I had to control my grief and move forever onward. These were the thoughts constantly pounding through my mind.

James' death started me to think deeply, perhaps for the first time in my life, and to read incessantly. I read *The Upanishads*, *The Tibetan Book of the Dead*, and *The Bible*. I studied the Greek historians and philosophers: Aeschylus, Aristotle, Epictetus, Herodotus, Plato, and Sophocles. I read works by Billy Graham, Dalai Lama, Deepak Chopra, Dr. Melvin Morse, and Dr. Raymond Moody, to name just a few. I devoured just about any book that dealt with the subject of reincarnation and life after death. *The New Testament* was the enlightened example to me that life is suffering, and you must force yourself through the pain and move forward.

Pain and suffering must be understood and fully absorbed. You cannot deaden the feelings. You cannot even attempt to understand life without suffering. The message I gleaned from *The Gospel of John* brought hope to me. Sometimes a spiritual transcendence can occur from experiencing intense sorrow.

What I understood for myself was disconcerting. Tragedy strikes everyone. Those who think they are immune, only have but to wait. It will come. More tragedy is lingering around the corner. Life is the great equalizer. You cannot barter for a better life. You must push on through tragedy with all the strength you have inside. Despite unanswered prayers, you must forever move forward and do what's right. To be alive is to have constant pain and struggle.

You must push yourself forward. You must pray. You must master discipline. You must keep focus. You must practice compassion. You must hone understanding. You must think. Learn to speak less, and listen more. Put others first and yourself second. Try to help as many people as you can in your life, and if you can't help them at least don't hurt them. The best possible life you can have is one of helping others, and constantly striving to do what is right, regardless of the outcome.

How do you know what is right? Search your heart. Buddha is about compassion; Jesus is about love. Put those together and it's pretty powerful. Treat everyone with dignity, respect, love, and compassion. The reward you receive is the knowledge and peace of mind that you did what was right.

I spent a career in the US Army continually taking and giving orders, and telling soldiers what to do. I came to an understanding that I could not control events. All I could do was try to lead a good life, help others, and set a positive example. I have failed over and over again. My joy comes from helping others when I can, and watching my children excel and lead good lives.

Now to the subject of my novels.

Writing the books *Sparrow's Tears, Close Your Eyes and See, Timeless Terror, Timeless Soldier, Timeless Embrace,* and *Timeless Destiny* became therapy for me — the best therapy. When I think of my son James, I see him always helping others — those who could not help themselves — whether at home or in school. He made me realize that nothing is without purpose; that there is a majestic plan which unfolds itself across the vastness of time equally embracing each life, no more or less important than another. Writing the novels became my way of honoring and paying tribute to James. It allowed me to envision him as an adult, giving him the type of life I would have wished for him. Writing the books allowed me to dream my son a life which I felt had ended too quickly. James Cenney is alive in the pages of my novels. He encourages my readers and me to move forever forward in life.

The hero of my novels — Captain James Ross — is patterned after my son. They both have the same looks, style, loves, and ambience. They are both heroes. But even more than that, as my son James Cenney would say, they "… are intelligent human beings."

My fervent hope is that veterans who are suffering from PTSD and depression can use fiction writing as therapy.

Bernard Cenney
Floresville, Texas

CLOSE YOUR EYES AND SEE

PART ONE

Do you see how God always hurls his bolts at the greatest houses and the tallest trees? For he is wont to thwart whatever is greater than the rest.

Herodotus
484 — 425 BC
Greek Historian

PROLOGUE

22 NOVEMBER 1963

It was a beautiful day as far as Texas days go.

The early morning hours had felt the dark dreary effects of a cold rain, but now the eerie chill was gone, and the sky beamed crystal blue and cloudless.

The sun was out emanating its warmth, and the streets were packed with enthusiastic throngs of people holding signs, cheering and waving.

The response of the citizens was tremendously positive as the motorcade slowly threaded its way down Main and approached Houston Street.

This political trip is going better than planned, he thought.

The Presidential limousine turned right onto Houston Street as the crowds of enthusiastic well-wishers started to thin out.

The response still remained overwhelmingly positive, and everyone in the motorcade started to relax and realize the worst was almost over.

Everyone, that is, except the United States Secret Service Special Agents.

They remained ever vigilant and attuned to any danger.

With eyes constantly scanning the crowds and buildings, they looked for any odd motion, any distraction that could be construed as a threat.

We're almost finished, he thought.

The last planned transition before the highway turnoff was approaching.

Very carefully the limousine lumbered slowly to the left and proceeded down Elm Street, maintaining its position in the motorcade.

The crowds had really thinned out now, as the highway could be seen up ahead.

People were scattered on the grassy areas to the left and right of the procession.

Some were snapping photographs and hand cranking their Polaroid cameras, while others were filming with their Kodak 8mm's.

But most were just cheering from the plaza and the many open windows of buildings paralleling the road.

Everything was going like clockwork.

BAM!

The sound was distinct as it sliced through the noise of the crowd.

What was that?

What was it?

We're on our way to the Trade Mart now, he thought to himself.

I don't see anything.

It must have been a firecracker.

BAM!

Something is wrong, terribly wrong!

The secure radio crackled: "Let's get out of here! We're hit! Get us to the nearest hospital quick!"

My God, he's hit!

What the hell!

No!

It can't be!

Do something!

Go!

Get over there!

Move it damn it!

Go!

Go!

Go!

BAM!

My God!

My God!

My God!

He was trained for such an emergency.

He knew what to do.

He had gone through countless scenarios before, over and over again.

Why didn't he move?

I need to get to the Boss!

Do something!

ANYTHING!

My God!

The motorcade sped away, and with sirens blaring raced towards the nearest hospital.

Within six minutes they arrived.

Chaos reigned.

He was stationed outside and waited.

He waited.

He waited.

He waited.

He heard people talking.

Rumors were spreading like wildfire.

Keep alert.

Keep alert.

This might not be over.

The double glass doors of the hospital emergency room opened.

A fellow Special Agent came briskly sprinting towards him to relieve him of his post.

His face was white as if all the blood was drained from it.

Every Secret Service Agent knew the President's code name was "Lancer." Members of his security detail also referred to John Kennedy as "the Boss."

"Lancer is gone, Pete," the Special Agent said quietly while catching his breath.

He couldn't comprehend what was being said to him.

"Say again," he hopelessly asked as his chest tightened.

"Say again."

The Special Agent looked at him with hollow eyes.

"He's gone. Lancer's gone," the agent said again softly.

He turned his head and looked towards the blood-soaked limousine.

A crowd of people started gathering and staring.

Nothing will ever be the same, thought US Secret Service Special Agent Peter Christianson to himself.

Nothing will ever be the same again.

PRESENT DAY

But I like not this great success of yours; for I know how jealous are the Gods.

Herodotus
484 — 425 BC
Greek Historian

CHAPTER ONE

CHANEL NO.5 AND CIGARETTES

With a dull, throbbing ache in the center of his skull reminding him he was still alive, Central Intelligence Agency Case Officer Randall Kloet slowly, agonizingly, mentally forced himself awake.

His eyelids fluttered and narrowly cracked open from what seemed like a thousand years of otherworldly sleep.

Concentrating, he forced his eyes to focus and took in the surrounding scene.

Beams of light crisscrossed in front of his face, but he could not tell if it was day or night, or how long he had been unconscious.

He could see a palm thatched ceiling and realized he was inside a room of some sort.

He was lying down and tried to rise, but failed.

The metal framed twin bed he was lying on creaked and groaned under his futile body stirrings.

He tried again and again to get up, but could accomplish nothing more than becoming frustrated over his inability to move his body.

He could not even turn his head to the side.

Kloet could feel some kind of sticky elastic tape pulling at the hairs across his left forearm, and shifted his eyes to see intravenous clear plastic tubing flowing from his arm to a medicine bag hanging from a pole towering above him.

The intravenous bag contained vecuronium bromide, a neuromuscular paralyzing drug.

Kloet could see, hear and feel, but could not move.

What the hell is going on?

Groggily, he recalled the events of last evening.

It seemed like the last night he had spent on earth.

Kloet remembered strolling down the streets in the waterfront area of Manila Bay.

Manila Bay in the Philippines is surrounded by the island of Luzon. To the right of the bay is the city of Manila, and to the left is the Bataan Peninsula.

Bataan.

The Bataan Peninsula will be forever remembered for the ninety day siege from January to April 1942, with the surrender of over seventy-five thousand Filipino and U.S forces during World War Two.

It was the largest surrender in United States history.

And who can ever forget the infamous Bataan Death March?

In April 1942, the 14th Japanese Imperial Army marched seventy-five thousand Filipino and US prisoners for ninety-seven kilometers to Balanga. Eleven thousand prisoners died along the way from malnourishment, disease, starvation, and torture. Those who could not keep up were savagely bayoneted and beheaded by the Japanese soldiers. The prisoners had been marched from Bataan by Japanese forces to prepare for the siege at Corregidor. The surrender at Bataan hastened the fall of Corregidor.

Corregidor.

That tiny island bastion, with its intricate network of subterranean tunnels and defensive armaments, fell to the might of the Japanese Imperial Army a month later on May 6th 1942.

Corregidor was eventually recaptured by Filipino and US forces in a brutal battle ending on the 26th of February 1945.

Today, the tiny tranquil island of Corregidor houses a solar powered lighthouse which illuminates the entrance to the ever mysterious and intoxicating South China Sea.

To the left of Bataan in the Zambales Province is Subic Bay, which once housed the largest United States Naval Base in the pacific.

Subic Bay US Naval Station was a major ship repair, supply, and rest and recreation facility for US servicemen.

However, both Clark US Air Force Base near Angeles City, and Subic Bay US Naval Station, were closed at the end of 1992. Partly because of the June 15th 1991 eruption of the volcano at Mount Pinatubo, just fourteen kilometers west from Clark Air Force Base, and thirty-seven kilometers north of Subic, but mostly because of the politics of Philippine President Corazon Aquino.

At Subic Bay is the wonderfully urbanized city of Olongapo, made famous over the years for selling custom jewelry to US Navy personnel.

Olongapo, meaning "head of the elder" in the Philippine language of Tagalog, got its name from an ancient popular legend of warring tribes and the decapitation of a wise old man who tried to bring the tribes together.

This night however, the waterfront area of Manila Bay was alive with brightly flickering red, yellow, and blue neon signs jockeying for the attention of a man's senses from the constant beeping of taxi horns, and the luxurious smells of Filipino cuisine wafting out of food stalls.

Kloet took it all in, and then around nine o'clock spied the Bamboo Hut Bistro near the Manila Yacht Club.

He entered the restaurant and was immediately swept up by a lovely young Filipino hostess sporting a name tag announcing her to be "Racquel."

Racquel was wrapped in a tightly fitting burgundy silk Chinese cheongsam dress. The dress was split at the right side all the way to her smooth thigh, with tiny gold embroidered buttons lining the left side up to the two inch high neck collar. A design of embroidered golden chrysanthemum flowers enticingly spread across her bosom. She wore four inch high heeled black open toed shoes, and no stockings. Her long straight black hair hung below her shoulders. Her lips pouted with a very wet pink colored lip gloss, and her broad cheeks had been brushed with a hint of rouge powder.

Smiling, Racquel handed Kloet a menu and spoke.

"Our special tonight is adobo chicken, sir," said Racquel.

Her long black hair fell over the dark brown pools of her eyes, and she brushed it back over her left shoulder with a flip of her hand.

Kloet quickly scanned the menu and settled on the adobo chicken special.

"Bring me a San Miguel beer and a glass of ice water as well sweetheart," said Kloet.

Racquel wrote down Kloet's order on her little notepad and shuffled away with a smile.

The food soon came, and Kloet was in heaven.

The adobo chicken was spectacular, with just the right amount of garlic and calamansi lime juice.

Kloet devoured every morsel, and then signaled Racquel for the check.

He paid the bill with fifteen dollars US and left a five dollar tip for Racquel.

Kloet stood up and stretched, and then walked out of the Bamboo Hut Bistro and into the musty Manila night air.

Still tasting the garlic in his mouth, he decided to stroll down Roxas Boulevard in search of a late night drink.

Soon he was past the Manila Yacht Club and starting to turn around, when he spotted a little nightclub with a brightly flickering red neon sign appropriately proclaiming it to be "Heaven on Earth."

Kloet smiled at the name and decided to stop in for a few beers before calling it a night.

As he pushed open the swinging door and walked inside, he was enveloped by melodies of classical music.

Interesting, thought Kloet.

He was expecting rock or pop music at the very least.

A Claude Debussy song was playing, one whose name he couldn't quite recall.

The club looked surprisingly quaint and elegant at the same time. It was dimly lit inside, except for a sparkling chandelier hanging from the center of the ceiling, surrounded by endlessly swirling cigarette smoke.

The club was jam packed full of bodies, with everything from businessmen looking for a last drink before heading home, to soldiers looking for evening companionship, to young couples looking to start the weekend early, to attractive female escorts just looking.

There were around ten small cocktail tables surrounding the center dance floor. To the left, a long teakwood bar jutted in front of and enveloped a huge wall-length mirror.

The bar immediately caught Kloet's eye and he started strolling over to it when a beautiful Filipino hostess spotted him.

The hostess glided over to him like an angel floating through the fog of the smoke filled club.

The hostess was very young, perhaps eighteen. She was trying desperately to look older, with too much rouge on her cheeks and a glistening gloss on her lips. A black cheongsam dress embroidered with a golden dragon crawling up the right side gripped her body with its claws. The cheongsam sported a high black collar, and had a thigh slit on the left side opening from the girls' ankle all the way to her bare waist. Highlighting the ensemble were four inch stiletto heeled black shoes, which tightly secured her tiny feet with red painted toenails.

Her dusky perfume permeated the air, and Kloet found himself immediately put at ease by her.

She led him to the bar where, pulling out a barstool to sit down, he told himself he would go back to his apartment after two San Miguel beers.

He always prided himself on his amount of self control and discipline.

Kloet was thirty years old with thinning, short cropped, chestnut brown hair. He wore circular wire rimmed glasses, spoke fluent Thai and Tagalog, and prided himself on staying in shape. He had grown up in Virginia, and graduated from the Pennsylvania State University majoring in history. Commissioned from ROTC, he spent several years in the United States Army as a Special Agent in counterintelligence before being recruited by the Central Intelligence Agency at Langley.

Now, he was a Case Officer serving in the cover position of Political Officer at the United States Embassy in Manila.

All his time was currently spent involved in Operation CAPACITY STRIKE.

CAPACITY STRIKE was the code name for the joint operation between the CIA and the military to counteract the terrorist activities of Abu Sayyaf, Jemaah Islamiyah, and Al-Qaeda operating in the southernmost Philippine Islands.

Kloet had been in Manila for the past two months, having transferred from the CIA Bangkok station.

He was only just beginning to know his way around the Philippines.

The first San Miguel came, and then the second.

Kloet drank them down slowly, and then paid his bar tab with US dollars.

He was starting to stand up when two soft, warm arms wrapped around him and pulled him down onto the barstool.

"Where are you going in such a hurry, sir?" asked the female owner of the arms.

Kloet looked at the woman.

She was young, about twenty-five years old.

The woman smelled of Chanel No. 5 perfume and cigarettes.

Her silky black hair was long and hung to her shoulders, accenting her face with bangs cut just above her eyebrows. Her face was classic Filipino with wide cheek bones, small petite nose, and soft brown skin. She wore a gloss which gave her large lips a full, scintillating, lustrous appearance. Her fingernails were painted with a clear polish and cut short. She was wearing a very short and tight little black dress, which was nearly transparent. Her natural height of five foot two was enhanced significantly by stiletto heeled glossy black shoes and muscled calves.

It was apparent she was a professional, and she arched her back and thrust out her chest while sitting down next to Kloet.

He had seen her before.

She had been walking the street outside the Bamboo Hut Bistro restaurant while I was eating, he thought.

And now here she was.

She was obviously a persistent escort.

"As much as I'd love to sweetheart, maybe you should find someone else down the bar. I'm ready to call it a night," said Kloet smiling.

The woman looked at Kloet.

She glided her right hand under the raven black hair that had fallen in front of her face and flipped it back and over her right shoulder.

The scent of her perfume floated into Kloet's nostrils and he let it fill his lungs.

She reached into her small black sequined purse and extracted a cigarette.

"Have you got a light, handsome man?" asked the woman.

Kloet smiled.

He had learned to always carry a pack of cigarettes and lighter, ever since he had attended the Basic Operations Course at the Armed Forces Experimental Training Activity years ago.

That was what the CIA Special Training Center was called at Camp Peary outside Williamsburg Virginia.

That's where he had learned to further hone the intelligence tradecraft skills the Army had taught him. Cigarettes and a lighter were a good way to break the ice and start any conversation. Either you smoked, or you didn't.

Kloet reached into his sports coat pocket and pulled out his Zippo lighter. His lighter had the seal of the US Embassy embossed on it.

He flipped open the cover and lit the young woman's cigarette.

The woman inhaled the smoke deeply into her lungs and then blew it out saying, "My name is Jupjang."

"That's a very pretty name. My name is Randal," said Kloet.

"Would you like a date tonight?" asked Jupjang.

"I'm sorry sweetheart, but I just can't. I've got an early day tomorrow," said Kloet.

Jupjang took another puff on her cigarette and said, "Are you sure? I'm a very good masseuse."

"Yes honey, I'm sure," replied Kloet.

Jupjang took another drag on her cigarette and looked discouraged.

"I understand, maybe later," she said.

Jupjang stabbed her cigarette out into the circular glass ashtray on the bar in front of her.

"Will you have one final drink with me and then walk me out of this place. I always hate to leave alone. Too many creeps out there," said Jupjang looking around.

"Surely," said Kloet.

Before Kloet could wave the man over, Jupjang was signaling the bartender for two more San Miguel beers.

"Beer always tastes better in a glass, don't you think?" said Jupjang.

"Clearly," said Kloet.

Jupjang got up and walked to the end of the bar where the glasses were stacked. On the way, she reached into her small purse and pulled out a perfume atomizer. She stopped in front of the glasses with her back to Kloet and pretended to spray some perfume on her neck. As she picked up the glasses, she sprayed the inside of one with what was in the atomizer.

The atomizer contained flunitrazepam, a powerful benzodiazepine hypnotic drug.

Jupjang turned around with the glasses and walked back to Kloet.

"Here you go, let me get that for you, handsome," said Jupjang, as she reached for the bottle of beer and poured it into Kloet's glass.

The alcohol would only exacerbate the effects of the hypnotic drug.

"Cheers," said Kloet, as he raised his glass and toasted Jupjang.

Jupjang picked up her glass and drank slowly as she watched Kloet finish half of his beer.

Kloet put his glass back down on the bar and stood up. He reached in his trousers pocket and pulled out ten US dollars and paid for the drinks.

Then he looked at Jupjang and smiled.

Kloet extended his arm, and Jupjang took it.

Together, they walked out of the Heaven on Earth nightclub and into the humid, misty Manila night.

"So where do you live?" asked Kloet.

Jupjang pointed with her finger.

"Just down the street and around the corner, in an apartment overlooking the alley in back," she said.

Together, arm in arm they walked past ancient shop windows with incandescently flickering neon signs illuminating their path.

The street was curiously alive with customers at this late hour, alive with the rich delicious aromas of mysterious Asian culinary delights, and the hustle and bustle noises of a never ending evening.

The climate in the Philippines was tropical monsoon. Monsoon rains were always pulled in by hurricanes, or, as called in the Pacific, typhoons.

It was typhoon season now.

The daytimes' high temperature, combined with the oppressive humidity and rainfall, created an evening fog that lazed down the streets and swirled around their legs.

The full moon leered at them through the vaporous mists.

Soon they turned the corner and were off of the main street and entering an alley.

They continued walking and had another thirty meters to go to get to the apartment that Jupjang called home.

Unexpectedly, Kloet recalled the name of the Claude Debussy song that was playing when he entered the nightclub.

The name of the song was *Tragédie*.

Kloet was gazing into Jupjang's face now with a quizzical look as he lost all feeling in his arms and legs.

"Just let it happen, darling," said Jupjang.

Then everything started spinning in front of his eyes, and with a dull throbbing pain in his head, Kloet pitched forward and fell face down into the stench of the narrow Manila back alley.

CHAPTER TWO

DREAMS OF DEATH

It was just after midnight.

The bewitching hour.

Lin Sparrow tossed and turned in her bed.

Sweat was beading on her forehead, and a low guttural moaning sound emanated from her throat and pushed through her lips.

Lin was asleep and dreaming.

It was the identical dream, night after night.

Night after night.

Night after night.

The dream always started the same way.

In her dream, the sun was setting over one of the many tiny islands in the Philippine chain, leaving its last gasps of brilliant red rays effervescing against the sparkling horizon.

The horizon intertwined with the sea and transformed it into a glittering bed of mermaids' diamonds.

The sea seduced and offered peace, tranquility, and surrender to the sands of the virgin white beach.

The beach was pristine and sprouted the occasional rough hewed palm tree groping skyward.

The palm trees swayed and lazily stroked the clinging moist tropical breezes that wrapped around and caressed the lighthouse.

The lighthouse was magnificent and provided a beautiful panoramic view of Subic Bay.

The dream continued.

The sidewalks were crowded with throngs of well-wishers clamoring for a last look at the motorcade as it lazily meandered on its way.

The crowds were looking at a young couple in the large long black limousine.

The handsome man wore a dark blue suit and necktie, with a white pin-striped shirt. The beautiful woman wore a pink skirted outfit with a pink pillbox-type hat.

The man brushed with his left hand at the shock of hair that always fell across his forehead. It stayed put for a second, then just fell back down again.

The woman held a dozen long stemmed red roses in a bouquet.

Both the man and woman waved cheerily to the crowds.

Lin knew the man.

He was James Ross.

Captain James Ross.

Green Beret officer James Ross.

James was her friend.

James was her lover.

The woman was Lin.

Lin Sparrow.

The couple was happy, content, and enjoying themselves.

BAM!

Suddenly, a shot rang out, piercing the tranquility of the scene.

It was an ear splitting, terrible, tragic gunshot blast.

Ross grabbed his throat and looked at Lin.

Lin was startled and reached out for her man.

BAM!

BAM!

As Lin held Ross, the third blast tore the top of his head off.

Brains, blood, and bone fragments splattered across Lin's face and body.

Ross crumpled into Lin's lap and she held him tight.

Why? She screamed silently in her dream.

Why?

Why?

Wet, sticky, metallic smelling blood covered Lin's clothes and body.

She was choking on the blood.

She wiped the blood out of her eyes.

Ross's blood soon poured out of the limousine and onto the beach.

The blood soaked the beach, transforming it into a crimson vermillion hell.

Out of this hell rose a creature of the night; a serpent; a devil.

Out of this hell rose Julius Creedmoor.

Creedmoor was the rogue CIA agent who had sold out his country to Abu Sayyaf.

Creedmoor was the demon who had tried to kill Ross and Lin in Kuala Lumpur last summer.

Lin watched as Creedmoor walked over to the limousine and held out his hand for her.

She turned away and continued desperately clutching Ross with tears running down her face.

Creedmoor reached out and grabbed Lin by her hair and violently jerked her head backwards.

Looking into her face, Creedmoor spewed forth his venomous words at Lin.

You are mine now woman! Creedmoor snarled.

Noooooooooooo!

Lin awoke at six o'clock in the morning with the jolt of an electric spark.

Her nude body was glistening from head to toe with trickles of salty sweat.

She kicked off the thin white bed sheet that had been covering her, and walked slowly into the small bathroom of her apartment, and clicked on the lights.

Lin examined her face in the large mirror hanging above the ancient porcelain sink.

This is crazy.

I've had the same dream over and over for weeks now.

Something is up.

Something is going to happen to James.

I can feel it.

I know it.

My father said I had the gift.

I've always had it.

Our neighbors called it witchcraft.

Others called it clairvoyance.

Whatever its name, I've got it.

I've got to do something.

I've got to find James before it is too late, she thought.

But why should I?

He left.

He went back to his Army life in the United States.

Then Lin started to rationalize.

He had to leave.

It's his job.

He's a soldier.

Slowly, the ugly specter of doubt entered Lin's mind, clawing at her psyche.

Doubt is the specter that we all have in our lives.

The specter of doubt leads us down the twisted and gnarled trails of fear, remorse, regret, ridicule, arrogance, and anger.

Agonizingly, the specter of doubt crawled across Lin's mind.

Maybe he's with another?

Maybe he has women everywhere, around the globe?

She stared deeply into the brown eyes analyzing her in the mirror.

Those are foolish thoughts.

I don't believe it.

James has always been troubled by the premature death of his father and mother.

He has always been troubled by the despair he sees in the world.

He has always been troubled when he sees good people suffer.

He has always been troubled when he sees evil doers triumph.

James sought out the answers from his faith.

His is the Christian faith.

His is the belief in the Christian God.

He questions why God would allow atrocities to occur rampant and flourish throughout the world.

Why does God allow innocents to be savagely raped and butchered?

Why does God allow children to be abused by the very institutions sworn to protect them and give them hope?

Why does God allow the existence of wars and disease, famine and murder, injustice and evil?

Why does God allow his greatest creation, human beings, to die?

James' faith is a great mystery to him.

His faith promises salvation if you just believe.

But what James came to understand, is that belief is not enough.

He realized that a human being has to act.

He realized that a human being has to create justice and truth, compassion and wisdom.

Most importantly, James realized that a human being has to act with love.

He realized there were three questions to answer in life.

What is worth dying for?

What is worth living for?

What is most precious in the world?

To James Ross, the answer he found was always the same.

The answer is love.

James tries to understand the spiritual and the mortal.

James is many things, thought Lin, *and I know what he is not.*

He is not a liar.

I've got two weeks leave coming from my Embassy job.

I'll take one.

But where will I go?

Lin stared back at herself in the mirror.

You know where, don't you?

You know exactly where to go.

The Philippine Islands, she told herself.

Lin worked at the United States Embassy in Kuala Lumpur.

Recently, she had been promoted from *Analyst and Interpreter,* to the position of *Executive Personal Secretary* to the Honorable Simon Watlington, the United States Ambassador to Malaysia.

But since the terrorist attacks in Kuala Lumpur last summer, Lin began reevaluating her career choice, and her life.

Her civil service job had been rewarding, but at a cost.

She experienced bureaucratic backstabbing and infighting; careerism and snobbery; pettiness and jealousy; gossip and hatred; manipulation and ineptitude; anger and downright stupidity.

She witnessed altruistic people get fired, and egotistic people get promoted.

And these attributes all seemed to occur daily in the confined office cubicles of the US Embassy.

She wanted something different, something fresh.

She wanted something that she could be proud of.

She wanted something that would make a difference in peoples' lives.

She wanted to give something of herself back to the people of Malaysia.

She wanted to have a sense of actually helping people, of making others' lives better off than they were.

She needed something more fulfilling than her current civil service government work.

So, she enrolled in an accelerated evening studies program at the Puteri Nursing College and completed her degree.

Now she was a registered nurse.

She had applied to work in the emergency room at the Twin Towers Medical Center in Kuala Lumpur, and was waiting for the right moment to tell Mister Watlington that she was resigning.

But now she had another issue: her dreams, her visions.

She needed to put the new job on hold and request leave from the embassy.

Mister Watlington will understand, she thought.

He'll let me go on a weeks' leave.

Mister Watlington will make it happen, she told herself.

Lin picked up her tube of Crest toothpaste and squeezed a dab out onto her pink toothbrush. She brushed her teeth quickly, and then gargled with a minty antiseptic mouthwash and spat out the residue into the sink.

She walked over to the shower stall and slid open the transparent glass door, stepping inside and closing it behind her. With hot water jets pulsating, Lin scrubbed herself in the steamy shower with an orange ginger body wash, and lathered her hair with Garnier Fructis shampoo.

She rinsed herself off thoroughly with tepid water, and then stepped out of the shower and dried herself off with a large red terrycloth towel.

Lin walked over to her teakwood dresser and creaked open the drawer.

She put on a sheer pair of panties and matching bra. Then she selected a white cotton knee length skirt and a sky blue blouse. She slipped a two baht gold chain with matching Buddha around her neck, and strapped a small gold Citizen watch with dark brown leather band onto her left wrist. She splashed Organza Indecence perfume on her neck, and rubbed her wrists together with a dash.

Lin looked at herself in the bathroom mirror.

She was five feet nine inches tall.

That was tall for a Malaysian lady.

But Lin was only half Malay.

She was a mixture of East and West, just like her boyfriend James Ross.

Her mother was Malay, and her father had been a British officer assigned to Kuala Lumpur. He had been killed from a terrorist bomb explosion when Lin was only three years old. She never really had gotten to know her father. Her mother had never remarried and kept the last name of Sparrow.

Lin continued staring at herself in the mirror.

Her silky, very dark brown hair cascaded slightly below her shoulders, with bangs in the front to her eyebrows. She had long brown eyebrows, and a petite nose that was slightly upturned. Her eyes were deep brown almonds that twinkled in the light, and her mouth was large and rather beautiful, with glistening full lips. Her skin was very smooth with almost no body hair. She kept her fingernails cut short and unpainted, but she did apply a clear polish to her toenails.

Lin reached down and picked up a cosmetic brush to apply a small trace of rouge blush powder to her Western cheeks.

When she was done, she looked around and slipped her feet into well worn, light blue, three inch heeled, stitched leather shoes.

Satisfied that she was finished, Lin walked through her apartment and unlocked the front door.

She walked outside and secured the door with a turn of her key, and then gracefully walked down a flight of stairs and out into the bright Kuala Lumpur morning.

The United States Embassy in Kuala Lumpur is located at number 376 Jalan Tun Razak, on the corner of Jalan Tun Razak and Jalan U-Thant Road intersections.

Lin did what she did every morning to get there.

She boarded the Putra Light Rail Transit System or LRT metro train, which took her from the end of her street to the Ampang Park LRT Station. It usually worked out to be about a twenty minute ride. Once at the Ampang Park LRT Station, the US Embassy was only a ten minute walk.

The LRT was on time today, as it always was. Kuala Lumpur transportation was the epitome of efficiency.

After the twenty minute ride, Lin exited the Ampang Park Station and walked the small distance to the Embassy.

She strolled up to the front gate on Jalan Tun Razak Road and stopped to show the uniformed Malaysian contract guard her laminated identification badge.

“Good morning Miss Sparrow,” said the armed security guard in the black uniform.

The security guard pushed a red button on his desk console, and a door in the eight foot tall steel mesh security gate swung open.

“Good morning,” said Lin as she walked through the secure access gate door and towards the Consular Section entrance.

Lin walked quickly up the concrete stairs and opened the blast resistant double paneled security doors, and allowed them to hiss closed behind her.

Walking into the vast ceramic tiled tomb of a lobby, her heeled shoes made a “*clip-clop, clip-clop*” sound.

She strode over to the security check-in station on the left and once again displayed her identification badge, except this time to a US Marine Corps guard.

Next, she swiped her card through a controlled access electronic scanning reader. The machine made a *“tweet”* sound and displayed a green light determining she had the proper clearance to continue.

Lin took the elevator to the third floor.

Exiting the elevator, she walked down the hall to the left and stopped in front of the huge steel door that controlled access to the Ambassador offices.

She lifted the hinged plastic cover off of the cipher lock on the door and punched in her secure access numbers. The cipher lock engaged, and with a tug on the handle the door opened. Lin allowed the door to close behind her with a metallic *“click”* and walked into the main outer office.

This office housed the Ambassador’s executive personal secretary.

This was *her* office.

Lin sat down in the large leather backed swivel chair behind her teakwood desk and powered up her official US computer.

The Dell Computer Company had won the contract several years ago, and was the computer of choice for the US Departments of State and Defense. The Information Management folks at the State Department had long ago established secure mainframe communications support throughout all US Embassies worldwide.

Lin inserted her identification card into the common access card or CAC reader and securely logged on.

She scrolled through her email message traffic, answering those messages that she could herself, and forwarding to the Ambassador what needed to be.

Then she reached for her black plastic STU III key and inserted it into the secure telephone unit third generation on her desk. Next, she turned the key clockwise establishing a secure electronic mode. Finally, she picked up the receiver and punched in the code numbers to check her secure messages.

Lin listened intently.

She only had three telephonic messages.

The first message was a reminder for the Ambassador to attend a private dinner tonight with the visiting US Secretary of Defense. The second was from the head of the US Agency for International Development to get on the Ambassador's schedule this week. And the third message was to remind Lin to remind the Ambassador that the Defense Attaché Officer would be in Singapore next week.

Lin typed reminders to all three messages into an email, and sent it off as an "eyes only" to the Ambassador with the press of a button on her Dell computer over the secure State Department encryption web.

Within thirty seconds, Ambassador Simon Watlington sent her a reply message.

Good morning Miss Sparrow, read the message.

Lin got up from her desk and approached the Ambassador's door.

She stopped and hesitated slightly, then knocked three times on the highly polished oak door.

"Come in," said Ambassador Watlington.

Lin opened the door and stepped inside the Ambassadors office.

The office sported a plush wall-to-wall burgundy tufted carpet with the symbol of the United States State Department woven into the center of it.

Nautical brass floor lamps in each of the four corners cast a warm, trusting glow about the room.

The walls were wood paneled in rustic cherry and adorned with ornately golden framed paintings of Victorian naval sea battles. The back wall was framed by a massive blast resistant bay window that overlooked the courtyard below.

In front of the bay window was the Ambassador's enormous teakwood desk. The desk was intricately hand carved with scenes of kimono draped oriental women, pagodas, bamboo forests, and flowers.

Behind the desk was a tall-backed oak chair with caster wheels on its legs, and upholstered in dark brown leather with brass rivets running down its sides.

In front of the desk were placed two similar looking chairs, but smaller in stature.

Behind these, in the center of the room, sat a large dark brown leather upholstered sofa and teakwood coffee table with glass inlays.

The Honorable Simon Watlington rose from his chair behind the desk and said, "Please, have a seat Miss Sparrow," motioning with his right hand for Lin to sit down.

Lin picked the chair to the right of the Ambassador and sunk down into it.

Simon Watlington was six foot four inches tall. He had been shaving his head to compensate for a receding hairline for years, and now was completely bald. He had thin, brown, over-arching eyebrows that seemed to resemble quotation marks on his forehead when he smiled. The left eyebrow was cut in half by a thin scar he received while fencing as a member of the Skull and Bones undergraduate society, decades ago, while at a Yale University competition. Watlington's eyes were jade green in color, which caused many people to stare at them unintentionally. His face was clean shaven, with the smell of Obsession aftershave.

Watlington was fifty-five years old, and enjoyed staying in shape. His weight hovered monthly between two hundred eighteen, and two hundred and twenty pounds. Exercise was a regular part of his day, and Watlington was considered a master of the Korean martial art of Hwa Rang Do.

He was a man who appreciated the finer things in life, and his left wrist was adorned with a Blancpain Fifty Fathoms chronograph wristwatch in stainless steel, with brown crocodile strap. The only ring he wore was a large Master Mason ring, with the square and compass symbols in 18 karat gold, on the third finger of his left hand.

Today, the Ambassador was immaculately dressed in a white three piece Armani suit.

"How are you, Lin?" asked Watlington

"Fine sir," replied Lin fidgeting in her seat.

"Well, what can I do for you today Lin?" asked Watlington.

Lin looked the Ambassador straight in his green eyes.

"Well sir, I am sorry for the short notice of this, but I really need to take a week of annual leave."

The Ambassador looked slightly surprised.

"When Lin?" he inquired.

Lin looked desperate.

"I'd like to start tomorrow, if I could, sir," Lin pleaded.

"Well of course Lin, anytime you want," said Watlington.

He paused, and then continued.

"Is everything all right Lin?" inquired Watlington.

"Yes sir, it's just that, well you see, I need some time to take care of some family issues," said Lin.

Watlington narrowed his gaze and examined Lin's face. He was a pretty good judge of character, and usually could tell if someone was telling the truth or not.

He had felt sorry for Lin ever since last summer when she got caught up, by accident really, in that regrettable terrorist affair at the Kuala Lumpur International Airport.

He also realized that Lin had become involved with that young Army officer, James Ross.

That was a shame.

Watlington had lost a reliable Abu Sayyaf contact over the incident.

That mission nearly blew his cover.

And now, as a result, his trusted CIA Case Officer, Julius Creedmoor, had decided to disappear, vanish, go rogue.

Watlington had had to answer a thousand questions over that incident to the State Department Board of Inquiry.

And then there was the Central Intelligence Agency Incident Review Board, which grilled him endlessly and actually tried to shift blame and lay it on *his* doorstep.

Well, Watlington would have none of it.

He defended himself and his actions.

After all, how could he be responsible if one of his Embassy staff officers sold out to Abu Sayyaf?

CIA had recruited the man.

They were the ones who guaranteed his loyalty to the United States.

They were the ones who were responsible.

They were the ones who had failed.

Watlington had made it a point, in all of his affairs, to tiptoe through the raindrops.

He was not a naïve man.

He did not see things as black and white.

To Watlington, issues were always gray.

Watlington enjoyed money and power.

He reveled in wielding both to his personal advantage.

He was on the periphery of intricate covert operations which his handlers considered essential.

He made sure the trail never led back to him.

Watlington was disappointed that Creedmoor had decided to run and was making his own deals now.

Creedmoor was acting without restraint.

Mostly though, Watlington was disappointed that Creedmoor lacked discipline and had decided to go rogue.

To Watlington, an undisciplined man was a liability.

And liabilities had to be dealt with quickly and cleanly.

Watlington leaned forward in his chair and looked at Lin.

He decided to ask her one final question.

"Where will you be heading off to on your leave, Lin?"

Lin thought about it a moment, and then replied, "The Philippines sir. I've got some family there which I haven't seen in a while."

Watlington leaned back in his chair.

He was not a fool.

He read the dailies.

He kept up to speed on all the intelligence summaries.

He knew Ross's friend, CIA agent Randal Kloet, had been abducted in the Philippines.

And now, this is exactly where Ross's girlfriend, Lin Sparrow, desperately needed to go on leave?

"I see, I see. Well, nothing like family is there Lin?" asked Watlington.

"Yes sir. So, would it be all right if I leave tomorrow sir?" asked Lin again.

Watlington leaned forward placing his forearms on the desk. He clasped his hands together as if in prayer.

He said, "No problem Lin. Take all the time you need. Do you think a week of annual leave will be sufficient?"

"Oh yes sir. A week is all I'll need," beamed Lin.

Watlington unclasped his hands and placed them flat on the desk top.

"Well, it's settled then. Just prepare the leave form and email it to me. I'll electronically sign it and you'll be off," said Watlington with a smile.

"Oh thank you sir. I really appreciate it," exclaimed Lin.

Lin rose up out of her chair, but Watlington remained seated.

"Think nothing of it Lin. Have a pleasant trip," said the Ambassador, smiling.

Lin smiled and turned around. She quickly walked out of the Ambassador's office and closed the door behind her.

Ambassador Simon Watlington sat still and continued to smile.

But then again, very few people in the world knew that he was not really the Honorable Simon Watlington, United States Ambassador to Malaysia.

Over thirty years ago while on a State Department assignment in Berlin, the real Simon Watlington had been terribly disfigured in a fiery car crash near Checkpoint Charlie.

That was the official newspaper account anyway.

The real Simon Watlington died in that accident.

That car crash had been planned and prearranged years before.

Simon Watlington had been chosen because he had no siblings, his father and mother were already deceased, and he was a junior Foreign Service Officer whose career could be manipulated.

The automobile accident scenario had been planned and set up for years in advance by a foreign intelligence service intent on having a long-term controllable asset deep inside the United States government.

The real Watlington's body was switched with the plastic-surgery-enhanced imposter in the counterfeit ambulance, and covered in bandages right down to the facial and vocal cord burn injuries.

With the face permanently altered, and the distinct vocal cord changes, who would be the wiser?

Any attempt at positive identification was physically impossible since the fingerprints had been burned off.

This imposter was now in place and being groomed for the highest of offices.

This *wolf in sheep's clothing* was a sleeper agent unknown to all except his handlers.

Unknown to all, except a select few.

Unknown to all, except Julius Creedmoor.

The smile left him as he reached over and picked up the STU III secure phone receiver.

He was going to make the most important phone call of his secret life.

CHAPTER THREE

ANY OTHER DAY

It was five o'clock in the morning.

Captain James Ross was extremely amused.

He had just woke up and finished putting on his official Army Physical Fitness Uniform, which consisted of a slate grey T-shirt which proclaimed "ARMY" in large black letters, and black running shorts also emblazoned with the word "ARMY," only in silver grey lettering.

I look like a recruiting poster, thought Ross.

He quickly flossed and brushed his teeth, and then gargled with an AAFES brand of mouthwash he had picked up at the local Army-Air Force Exchange Store. After he could stand the stinging antiseptic in his mouth no longer, Ross leaned forward and spat out the mouthwash into the white porcelain bathroom sink.

He raised his head and looked up into the mirror above the sink.

He looked into the piercing eyes, dark brown eyes that were half Thai and half American, half East and half West.

Then he looked at the shards of hair hanging in front of his eyes and frowned.

Franticly, he ran his fingers through his thick shock of hair and tried to push the dark brown bangs back off his forehead.

After two seconds they just fell back down in more disarray.

Oh the hell with it, he thought.

Ross walked into the kitchen and gave the stove a quick glance to make sure it was turned off. His mother, God rest her soul, had always insisted he double check the stove before leaving their home. He told her one time, "Mom, we're all going to be gone on vacation, and you'll still be here checking the stove."

It was a habit he never forgot.

He hurried to the front door and, looking around, gave the apartment one more quick glance over.

"Too much time spent in counterintelligence," he muttered to himself.

He turned off the lights and walked outside locking the front door behind him.

Ross resided in the great northwest city of Steilacoom, in Washington State.

He rented a second story apartment on Rainier Street, within a stones' throw of Jakes Bar and Bistro, overlooking Puget Sound.

He loved the sights, sounds, smells and tastes of living near the sea. It seems his senses could never get enough of it: the mysterious ships silhouetted on the horizon, the sharp clanging of nautical bells in the distance, the lapping of the waves against the wharfs, the musty smell of flotsam and jetsam on the beaches, and the aromas of fine seafood cuisine wafting through the midnight fog.

He loved everything about it.

Ross quickly bounded down the two flights of twisting stairs and briskly walked across to his car.

He kept his ancient automobile keys securely fastened to his U.S. Army issued dog tag chain around his neck.

Gingerly, he pulled the chain up and over his head.

Carefully guiding the key into the lock, he turned it clockwise until the door knob rose shakily with an audible *"pop."*

He opened the left side drivers' door and squished down on the cold vinyl of the ivy gold colored threadbare bucket seats.

Leaning forward, he slid the ignition key in and turned it to the right until the engine caught with a roar.

With his left hand, he released the hand parking brake under the dashboard by pulling it out slightly, and turning it down and to the left, while gliding it forward.

Confidently, he pressed twice on the throttle with his right foot, giving the car some fuel, before cautiously depressing the black release button on the floor automatic shifter and engaging it into reverse.

Ross backed out ever so carefully to avoid scratching the Nissan's and Volvo's that always seemed to park too close to him.

He depressed the black release button once again and shifted into drive.

Carefully, he steered the car through the parking lot mouse trap maze and out into traffic.

Ross drove south down Rainier Street and turned left onto Union Avenue. Once on Union, he drove south again until he came upon DuPont-Steilacoom Road. He always drove down DuPont-Steilacoom Road to get to Fort Lewis, or Joint Base Lewis-McChord, as it was now named from the combining of Fort Lewis with McChord Air Force Base.

Ross's pride and joy was his car, a 1968 Ford Mustang fastback.

He was taking the car through its paces now, and driving hard and fast towards Fort Lewis.

The fastback was handling well, with the luminescent needle fluttering unwaveringly at seventy miles an hour behind the scratched plastic face of the speedometer gauge.

The forty-four year old Mustang was barely showing its age as Ross held the steering wheel firm and pushed the small 200 cubic inch six cylinder engine ever onward.

The antique car had long ago lost its immunity to road noise, and even a leisurely drive made Ross's ears feel as if he were experiencing the roars of the Indianapolis Motor Speedway. The muffler had recently, somehow, become punctured, and the result was a throaty and booming sound that gave the car a hot rod stylish ambiance.

Ross fiddled with the archaic AM radio trying to find a station without much static.

He finally settled on a Frank Sinatra song, and sat back to enjoy the ride.

It suddenly started to rain, as it always did, in Washington State.

The predictable downpour caused Ross to turn on the windshield wipers to clear his view.

The rain sloshing over the Mustang caused its original faded lime gold paint to effervesce into an antique green patina.

As the wipers were doing their job, the rainy onslaught seemed to end as quickly as it had started. Now there was only a fine mist running off the windshield with flowing streams wistfully winding their way across the hood.

Ross was always cautious.

He realized his old Mustang could develop a multitude of mechanical problems at any time and leave him stranded on the road.

He surmised that deep down inside, psychologically, he was in love with that thrill.

How absurd, he thought.

Most other officers he knew drove BMW's or Mercedes. But he loved this old fastback and could never imagine himself driving anything else.

Ross was soon approaching the front gate of Fort Lewis United States Army Installation.

He saw the front gate reduced speed limit sign, and slowed down to ten miles an hour.

As he drove up and over the speed bump, Ross leaned forward reaching into his back pocket and pulled out his Velcro olive drab wallet.

The young female civilian contract security guard at the front gate looked at Ross as he struggled to manually roll down the passenger side window.

Ross held up his laminated US Army identification card for the security guard to see.

"Doesn't that car have power windows?" the security guard asked.

"Nope," said Ross. "No power windows, no power brakes, no power steering, no power seats, no CD player, no GPS."

"Awesome. That's really retro," said the female security guard. "Is it a '65?"

"No," said Ross. "It's a 1968."

"Wow. That's cool. Is it for sale?" inquired the security guard.

"No," replied Ross. "I'd sooner sell myself."

"I wish I had one. Take care Captain," said the security guard, and she waved him on through.

Ross put his ID card back inside his wallet and rolled up his window. He carefully drove through the security gate area.

As the Mustang pulled away, the young female security guard raised an eyebrow and whispered to herself, "How much honey?"

Ross drove skillfully and determinedly as he headed towards the 1st Special Forces Group Headquarters.

1st Special Forces Group was the United States Army unit that Ross had been assigned to for the past three years.

Two of those years had been spent as the Commander of an Operational Detachment Alpha, or ODA.

This last year saw Ross completing his staff time as the senior staff intelligence officer, otherwise known as the Group S-2.

Ross had been selected by the Group Commander to be the S-2, even though the position was considered senior staff and normally required an officer in the rank of Major to fill it.

He spent most of his time interfacing with national agencies on special operations matters, and a great deal of time traveling to the Group's area of operations which comprised the Southeast Asian basin.

His S-2 staff office, or intelligence section, was manned by a senior Master Sergeant and three other veteran operators.

Ross was single and could spend as much time as needed at the unit or traveling.

The more overseas he traveled, the more he was steered towards making the Army a career.

He had never felt better about his choice of profession.

He loved his job and his life.

Soon Ross was motoring around the 1st Group Headquarters parking lot and found his designated S-2 parking spot.

He pulled in and turned off the engine.

Getting out of the fastback, Ross looked at his wristwatch.

Ross's watch was a Benrus military type. His grandfather had been issued the Benrus and worn it as an Infantry Sergeant in the Americal Division throughout the Philippines Campaign during the Second World War.

Grandpa Ross had passed the Benrus on to him, as a graduation present, during his Army ROTC commissioning ceremony at Texas Christian University years ago.

All of Ross's grandparents were now deceased, and he never even had a chance to know his Thai grandparents. But the time he had spent with his American grandmother and grandfather in Pennsylvania had always been very special to him.

The Benrus was one of Ross's treasured possessions.

Ross's Benrus had become water-logged last summer when he had to parachute into the Strait of Malacca during a routine training conference which had turned into a counterterrorist nightmare.

As soon as he got back to the States, Ross had the Benrus thoroughly cleaned and well oiled. Now it again functioned flawlessly. Its luminescent hands displayed five-thirty in the morning.

Not bad, thought Ross.

Soldiers were milling around and gathering into their respective groups to go through the daily morning ceremony and conduct calisthenics.

The first part of the ritual consisted of standing at attention and saluting while raising the flag as an instrumental version of *The Star Spangled Banner* song was broadcast over the compound.

The second part involved participating in physical training, or PT, as it was better known.

Ross remembered back, years ago, when his father told him that his battalion used to stand at attention for the song, *Ballad of the Green Berets,* played right after the National Anthem. The official PT uniform back then was bright yellow sweat pants and jacket, affectionately referred to as "the banana suit." Although that uniform was issued, SF didn't utilize it and soldiers used to exercise in whatever clothes they wanted to wear.

But that was on the island of Okinawa.

That was a long time ago.

Things seemed simpler somehow back then.

Those were different times, thought Ross.

No sense dwelling on the past.

I live now.

Ross scanned the gathering of soldiers and saw Master Sergeant Jeremy Clark.

Clark was Ross's Non-Commissioned-Officer-In-Charge.

Everyone called Clark by his initials "JC."

"Good morning sir," said Master Sergeant Clark standing to attention and snapping out a smart salute.

Ross smiled and returned the courtesy.

"Morning JC. Where are the guys?" inquired Ross.

"Right over there, sir," said Clark, motioning sideways to the right with his head.

Ross turned his head and looked at his men.

Along with Master Sergeant Clark, Ross was in charge of three other men in his S-2 shop. They were Sergeant First Class Rufus Hatcher, Sergeant First Class Clifton Hammett, and Staff Sergeant Stuart O'Leary. All were experienced Special Forces Operators. Ross was extremely proud of them all.

The three men saw Ross and quickly surrounded him in a circle.

Ross laughed, "What the hell?"

"Perimeter security, sir," laughed Sergeant Hatcher.

"Just securing you from any trouble, sir," snorted Sergeant O'Leary.

"Last time we let you alone you almost single handedly destroyed Malaysia, sir," chuckled Sergeant Hammett.

Ross remembered last summer.

How could he ever forget?

He saw the scars every time he looked in the mirror.

"Yeah, where were you guys when I needed you?" laughed Ross.

At five minutes before six o'clock in the morning, the milling around suddenly halted.

All soldiers mechanically formed into their respective team, company, and battalion ranks. The resulting professional formation was straight out of the drill and ceremonies manual of West Point Military Academy.

Ross's men filed in with the Group Headquarters enlisted staff.

Ross stood at attention in the front of the formation with the other senior staff officers.

The senior staff officers consisted of the S-1, S-2, S-3, S-4, and S-5. These staff sections represented personnel, intelligence, operations and training, logistics, and civil-military affairs.

Colonel Fred Gautier, affectionately referred to as *the old man,* was the Group Commander of all of these magnificent soldiers. He had served in this position for just under two years, and was getting ready to retire in three months. But he still had a few weeks left before he started his out processing, and he was trying to tie up loose ends.

The ranks were a little thin this morning. 2nd Battalion was overseas to Iraq in Combined Joint Special Operations Task Force — Arabian Peninsula, and 3rd Battalion was deployed to Combined Joint Special Operations Task Force — Afghanistan. 4th Battalion had just activated a few months before, and was still short of men. Despite this, there were over three hundred Special Forces soldiers present in this early morning formation.

Colonel Gautier took his place and called his soldiers to attention.

The Colonel did an about face and, as the National Anthem played, raised his right arm rendering a perfect salute towards the ascending American flag.

Over three hundred men followed the Commander's example.

What a sight to behold, thought Ross as he saluted.

At the end of the ceremony, Colonel Gautier ordered his subordinate commanders to, "Take charge of your units and conduct PT."

Soldiers received their commands and started to fall out of the formation.

It was the same as any other day.

As personnel were starting to break up into running formations, Colonel Gautier looked at Ross and the rest of his senior staff and motioned with his hand for them to follow him to his office.

I wonder what's up, thought Ross.

This is unusual.

The old man usually runs PT and waits until the daily o-nine-hundred staff meeting before putting out any information to the sections.

Ross could feel his heartbeat speed up.

CHAPTER FOUR

MESSAGE OF DEATH

Adjacent to the Group Commanders office is a conference room. Inside the room is a large oblong mahogany table which had to be at least fifteen feet long. Six tall black leather swivel chairs lined each side, with three chairs on the far end opposite the Group Commander's larger adjustable black leather swivel chair on the other end. On the surface of the table was a quarter inch of protective glass. In the center of the glass lay a tray holding a steaming pot of coffee. Surrounding the coffee pot sat the coffee mugs of the senior staff officers.

Ross and the other officers quickly found their designated spots around the table and stood at the position of attention.

Colonel Gautier slumped down into his chair.

"Take your seats gentlemen," he said.

Colonel Gautier was showing his age.

He had just turned fifty-two years old, and his closely cut gray hair was thinning out. His face was worn and weathered, and displayed the intense daily stress he was under.

Stress induced from being responsible for, and commanding, well over one thousand soldiers conducting special warfare on a global scale.

He leaned back in his chair and looked around the conference room at the faces of his staff.

He gazed into the five sets of faces staring intensely back at him, waiting for his slightest utterance.

Warrior faces?

No, not hardly.

Colonel Gautier never used the word, *warrior*.

He hated the word.

To Colonel Gautier, the word *warrior* had no reason to exist in this world, or the next.

He thought the Army was wrong in implementing *that word* to describe soldiers.

It was an example of political correctness turned around at its worst.

In his mind, the word *warrior* conjured up images of brutal Vikings or barbarians raping and pillaging, looting and murdering.

Certainly not a title any real soldier wanted to be known by.

During World War Two, the United States Armed Forces operated under the heading of *War Department.* After that devastatingly world changing war was over, the name was changed to *Department of Defense,* a gentler, softer sounding title.

More politically correct for the times.

Now, some knucklehead got the idea to call soldiers "warriors" in some misbegotten idea of disguising the terrors of war with a word.

They were substituting style for substance again.

As if calling a soldier by the term "warrior" made them somehow psychologically feel more aggressive, or more deadly, or, God forbid, more special.

Being labeled "a warrior" was adding to the psychological torment of those suffering with PTSD, or Post Traumatic Stress Disorder. That label created unrealistic expectations in mentally stressed soldiers' minds. After all, the Army called you a warrior, so you had to act like a warrior, didn't you?

Soldiers should be called what they are — Soldiers.

The word warrior was straight out of some arcade video game with flash-bang sounds and realistic looking plastic weapons.

War was not a video game to be scored and applauded.

War was the single most indescribably terrible act mankind ever devised.

War was a last resort, after all diplomacy had failed.

If it had to be war, then it had to be engaged rapidly, and finished as aggressively and quickly as possible.

Being a soldier was noble and respected.

Being a warrior was crazy.

Nobody in their right mind ever wanted to go to war, least of all soldiers.

Real soldiers hated war.

Real war was not the fantasy as portrayed in the movies on the silver screen.

There were no winners, only those who lost, and those who lost more.

Fred Gautier had been on too many battlefields, and held too many wounded friends in his arms, feeling their last dying breaths on his face, to think any differently.

He hated war.

He realized that wearing his uniform meant he was an instrument of United States foreign policy.

He prayed that cooler heads would always prevail to prevent war.

He always had a conflict in his mind about what war really was.

He had studied war at the United States Army Combined Arms Center at Fort Leavenworth Kansas, while he was attending the Command and General Staff Officers Course.

He knew about conventional warfare and unconventional warfare; strategic warfare and tactical warfare; guerrilla warfare and counterinsurgency.

He knew as much about making war as McDonalds knew about making hamburgers.

But all he really knew is that he had friends he would never see again, because of war.

They were dead.

They were never coming back to life.

They had been blasted apart on some forgotten battlefield thousands of miles away, while the rest of America went on vacations and worried about the price of gasoline.

Less than one percent of the American population had ever served in the military and less than ten percent even knew someone personally who had served.

Heroism was something thrust upon you, on the battlefield.

Heroism was something old men wrote about in history books.

He figured everyone wearing the uniform was heroic.

In his mind all soldiers, whether unconventional special operators or conventional troops, were professional.

He considered them all to be dedicated men and women keeping America safe.

They were all volunteers these days.

They all put themselves in harms' way for their country.

They were quiet professionals who never boasted or bragged about their profession.

This new *warrior* identity was another way the Army was pushing style over substance.

A shoot at anything that moves undisciplined mentality was what got your own soldiers and civilians killed.

He hoped to God that Basic Training would produce quality, professional, competent soldiers.

He wanted to serve with *soldiers,* not *warriors.*

Go figure out that one, Sun Tzu!

Everybody was a *warrior* now.

Whenever training corners were cut, the product was always poor, and put soldiers' lives at risk.

Tough, aggressive, realistic military training was the only answer to producing a qualified soldier.

This new warrior personality was a modern trend.

Well, thought Colonel Gautier, *I never was a trend setter.*

These were soldiers' faces looking at him.

These faces belonged to determined men.

These were quiet, professional men.

These were his men.

These were men who would do anything for their Commander.

These were men who would do anything for *the old man.*

It was hard for anyone who never wore the uniform to understand what sacrifices all soldiers made.

How could you ever explain to your wife that you could be uprooted at a minutes' notice and sent to war?

How could you ever explain to your wife why you moved from one military post to another military post every two years, while her civilian friends stayed put in one place all their lives?

How could you ever explain to your wife why you are forty-five years old and don't own your own home yet, because you will move next summer?

How could you ever explain to your children why they had to be uprooted out of school at Christmas time because you just received official orders to move to a new post?

How could you ever explain to your children why you had to buy their clothes second hand at the post thrift shop instead of downtown at the mall because you could not afford it?

How could you ever explain to your teenagers why they could not go to the best colleges because your salary was so small?

How many births, and birthdays, and anniversaries would you miss throughout your career because you were deployed overseas?

How could you ever explain to your wife that congress was cutting the budget and you would not be promoted to the next rank?

How could you ever explain to your wife why YOU weren't promoted and someone else was?

How could you ever explain to your wife the shame you felt when you left the service without the benefits of a retirement?

How could you ever explain to your wife that a "toxic" commander destroyed your chances at promotion with a pen stroke on a single piece of paper?

How could you ever explain to your wife that your career was destroyed because someone had the commanders' ear and you didn't?

How could you ever explain to your wife about the politics and back stabbing that occurred among the higher ranks?

One time a Special Forces Sergeant Major told him that he saw the officer corps as "…a bunch of rats on a sinking island. They were all going to die, but they kept clawing and biting each other to be the last one to perish."

He always thought that was keen NCO insight.

He had always tried his best throughout his career to take care of all of his soldiers and their families.

There was always some underlying reason for soldiers who had problems.

He had always tried his best to understand every situation and mentor every soldier personally.

He never threw a soldier away.

Some commanders felt they didn't have the time to spend on what they considered "substandard" soldiers.

Not Gautier.

He took the time to try to salvage every soldier he could.

He knew all people had issues.

It was Gautier's job as their commander to help them.

Unlike some of his colleagues, who were only out for their own personal aggrandizements, he considered it his job to make his soldiers successful.

He wondered what Al-Qaeda thought when they saw on television and read in the newspapers how we destroy each other.

He looked at his soldiers as if they were his own children.

He would correct them at times, but never ever throw one away.

He wanted them all to be successful and turn out better than him.

That is one reason why his men all supported him.

That is the reason his men all followed him.

He hated when a stigma shadowed a soldier over their whole career.

Jesus Christ, he thought, *was there no redemption?*

Why would an officer choose a specific soldier to destroy their career?

Usually, it was because the officer was jealous, envious, or just plain mean spirited.

Were there bad, maladjusted officers in the Army?

Sure there were, just like in any other large corporation.

They had the power to destroy a soldiers' life before it even began.

Many Special Forces soldiers thought outside the box with unconventional insight.

Many officers could not grasp this notion.

He hated when he read on an evaluation report: *Does not belong in the Army; does not belong in Special Forces.*

All that told him was that the writer, usually an officer, was himself a failure in leadership and should not be in the Army or Special Forces.

Special Forces soldiers had to be unconventional, unorthodox, quick thinking, and adaptable in every situation. Any officer who could not appreciate that, or who wrote such comments, was just plain stupid.

Colonel Gautier shifted his gaze to the stack of folders which had been placed neatly in front of him. Folders which carried intelligence summaries and the latest daily classified message traffic of importance to the mission of 1st Special Forces Group. On the front of the top folder was stapled a classification sheet proclaiming "SECRET" in large red letters at its top and bottom. He picked up this folder and opened it, shifting through its contents. When he found what he was looking for, he put on his reading glasses.

Ross reached forward and poured himself a cup of coffee, then relaxed back in his chair.

"Gentlemen, there has been an incident involving Operation CAPACITY STRIKE," said Colonel Gautier grimly.

Ross stopped sipping his coffee in midstream and put down his cup.

Colonel Gautier said, "As you know, CAPACITY STRIKE is our joint operation with the Central Intelligence Agency to counteract the terrorist activities of Abu Sayyaf, Jemaah Islamiyah, and Al-Qaeda operating in the southernmost Philippine Island of Mindanao and the Sulu Archipelago."

Ross knew about CAPACITY STRIKE. He had worked with CIA Case Officers on that operation in the past. His best friend, Randal Kloet, had just recently transferred from Bangkok to the CIA station in Manila and was actively engaged in that mission.

Ross held his breath.

Colonel Gautier continued.

"One of the Case Officers assigned to CAPACITY STRIKE was abducted last night. Abu Sayyaf has already claimed responsibility and sent a ransom demand to the US Ambassador in Manila. Seems a DVD was sent showing a Case Officer named Randal Kloet held hostage. They are demanding all Abu Sayyaf, Jemaah Islamiyah and Al-Qaeda terrorists held in Philippine prisons to be set free."

Colonel Gautier let the information set in for a second.

He continued.

"The demands further state that if the prisoners are not released in ninety-six hours, Kloet will be beheaded, with the remains delivered to the steps of the American Embassy in Manila."

There was silence around the briefing table.

Colonel Gautier said, "The Philippine military and police are actively searching for Mister Kloet, but as we all know, ninety-six hours is not much time."

Ross was stunned.

"Well, that's all gentlemen," said Colonel Gautier as he rose from his chair.

All the senior staff immediately stood up and remained at the position of attention, waiting for the Colonel to depart the area.

But he did not leave.

Instead, Colonel Gautier looked around and said, "Captain Ross I want to see you for a second. Everyone else is dismissed."

With that, the rest of the senior staff officers filed out of the conference room.

CHAPTER FIVE

UNOFFICIAL MISSION

Ross waited for the Colonel to sit down before taking his seat.

Colonel Gautier looked at Ross and said, "I wanted to talk with you privately about this, son. Listen Jim, I know you are friends with Kloet. I know you are good friends. I'm sorry this happened, but there's nothing we can do."

Ross asked, "What about the State Department? Have they engaged their Diplomatic Security guys on this? They have investigators and hostage rescue teams."

Colonel Gautier shook his head negatively and frowned.

"They are doing all they can, son," said Colonel Gautier, not believing what he was saying himself.

Ross asked, "What about SFOD-Delta? Have they been alerted? What are they doing?"

Colonel Gautier said, "They would act if they could, but ninety-six hours is not much time without any strong intelligence. I don't have to tell you this, you already know it. Hell, even Charlie Company in 1st Battalion would strike if they knew where to strike."

Ross lowered his head and shook it. Then he looked up into Colonel Gautier's face.

"What else do we know sir? What information have you personally got, sir?"

Colonel Gautier took off his reading glasses and looked into Ross's face; the face that he had sent throughout Southeast Asia on numerous missions in the past; the face that now displayed scars from last summer while on a Malaysian mission with Kloet.

Colonel Gautier revealingly said, "What I found out, from my contacts in the US Embassy in Manila, is that Kloet was abducted in retaliation for the killing of Jamal Mahlik Aisha."

Ross couldn't believe it.

Jamal Mahlik Aisha was the cell leader and senior member of Abu Sayyaf that Ross himself had eliminated in Kuala Lumpur last summer.

Now Ross's best friend, Randal Kloet, was going to be murdered because of Ross's own actions.

Ross looked at the floor thinking, and then slowly looked up into the Colonel's face.

Quietly, professionally, Ross said, "Sir, I have to go there."

Colonel Gautier immediately held up his hands as if to halt him.

"Whoa, hold it Jim. I know how you feel, believe me. But I can't let you go. We have no charter for this."

Ross pleaded, "Sir, no one is going to do anything. You and I know our government does not negotiate with terrorists. Without valid intelligence to act on, they will let Randal Kloet die."

Colonel Gautier looked understandingly at Ross. He said, "I did find out something else, confidentially."

Ross moved forward onto the edge of his chair.

Colonel Gautier said, "I found out that Kloet is being held in an Abu Sayyaf stronghold on Jolo Island in Indanan Township. That's all my embassy contact in the Philippines could tell me. He didn't even have a precise location, only somewhere on the island. That information has also been verified by what the boys at the National Security Agency could determine from voice intercept operations."

Now Ross at least knew where to look.

Colonel Gautier said sternly, "Look, I'm retiring in less than three months. I start out processing in two weeks for Christ's sake! The Army, in all their wisdom, won't let me stay any longer. It's part of the damn drawdown of officers again. We go through it at the end of every war. Congress says they are balancing the budget. I myself call it the dumb-downing of the Army, personally."

Ross looked at Colonel Gautier. His face tightened and displayed a determination that Colonel Gautier knew only too well.

Colonel Gautier's expression softened. He said, "All right, all right son. What do you want to do?"

Ross answered, "Let me catch a flight immediately out of SEATAC for Manila. I've developed dozens of contacts over the last couple of years in the Philippines. Let me access them and find out exactly where Kloet is being held. Once I do, I'll forward the information directly to you sir, and it can then be placed into the proper channels. SFOD-Delta can act, or Charlie Company. That's all I'm asking for, sir. Just let me gather validated intelligence for a hostage rescue operation to be mounted."

“That’s all, huh? That’s all you want? Only that?” asked Colonel Gautier dumbfounded.

“Sir, Kloet is my friend. He saved my neck on more than one occasion. He has helped 1st Group out many times, and given us HUMINT far beyond what we were entitled to receive, sir,” said Ross.

“There’s just not enough time, son. Not enough time,” said Colonel Gautier shaking his head negatively.

“Sir, let me try,” imploringly asked Ross.

Colonel Gautier shook his head and said, “God damn it, God damn it. We don’t have the authority for this. We have not been given the mission.”

“Sir …”

“And I could be court-martialed and sent to Leavenworth Penitentiary for this. And you, you could be killed. What would I tell your family?”

Ross’s father and mother had died years ago. He had no one else.

“Randy Kloet is my family, sir,” replied Ross.

That comment, from any other officer, would have sounded corny to Colonel Gautier, but not from Ross.

Ross was different.

Ross was always serious, while others just went through the motions.

Many officers just punched their tickets and moved from assignment to assignment as quickly as possible to get promoted.

Not Ross.

Ross stayed as long as he could in field assignments with soldiers.

He believed in getting his hands dirty.

He believed in leading from the front.

He believed in what he was doing.

Colonel Gautier knew Ross's father and mother were deceased, and he was their only child. Gautier and his wife had tried to have children themselves, but three pregnancies resulted in two miscarriages and one stillbirth, and a thousand regrets. Over the past two years, Gautier had sort of, unofficially, adopted Ross.

Colonel Gautier looked away and squinted, trying to suppress the emotions attempting to overtake him.

Ross replied, "Sir, I am your S-2, your senior intelligence officer. All I will be doing is gathering intelligence to try and save a fellow intelligence officer's life."

Silently, Colonel Gautier brought his hands up to his face. He closed his eyes and rubbed them with his fingers. He squeezed his eyes shut underneath his palms as if the problem would disappear when he opened them. Slowly, he pulled his hands down from his face and looked at Ross.

"All right," said Colonel Gautier.

"All right, as my S-2, I am sending you on orders, officially unofficial, to Manila today. Access and engage your intelligence assets to find out what you can about the hostage situation. Send message traffic to me securely as soon as you get anything."

"I'll give you ninety-six hours."

Ross's face was stoic.

"After ninety-six hours, you come home," said Colonel Gautier.

Ross stood at attention and saluted *the old man.*

"Yes sir," said Ross.

He executed an about face and quickly walked out of the commanders conference room.

Ross headed for his S-2 office where he kept a carry-on suitcase emergency packed for just such a situation.

Colonel Gautier grabbed the arms of his chair and pushed himself up and out.

He walked off towards the S-3 section to tell the officer in charge to put Ross on immediate orders to the Philippines today.

Ross had his NCOIC, Master Sergeant Clark, drive him as fast as he could to Seattle-Tacoma International Airport.

Once at SEATAC, Ross breezed through security with his orders in hand and his US official passport.

Ross had to scramble to get on flight 2266 by nine o'clock, but he made it and was on time to board the Alaska Airlines De Havilland DHC-8 plane.

The De Havilland DHC-8 turboprop aircraft took him to Vancouver British Columbia.

Once in Vancouver, Ross transferred to flight 839 of Cathay Pacific Airlines to fly on an Airbus A340 jet airliner nonstop to Hong Kong.

After he arrived in Hong Kong, he boarded his final flight, a three hundred passenger Cathay Pacific Boeing 777 jumbo jet to the Philippines.

Ross arrived in Manila at midnight, a full day later than when he left the United States.

He was exhausted.

CHAPTER SIX

ENTER MANILA

The Ninoy Aquino International Airport was crowded as usual. It was jam packed with Filipinos, Chinese, Japanese, Malaysians, Vietnamese, Indonesians, Thais, and just about every other nationality in Southeast Asia.

The Filipino and English languages were both freely spoken here, by the ninety-two million people who inhabited these seven thousand islands.

The Philippines was rich in the cultural traditions of Malay, Hindu, Muslim, and Christianity. Manila itself was ninety percent Christian, and ten percent Muslim. Jolo Island, on the other hand, was the exact opposite.

There was a huge line of at least two hundred people waiting to get through customs. Business men, missionaries, soldiers, students, families, and tourists were all biding their time.

Ross marked time as well, patiently.

After about an hour, he was through customs and outside looking for a taxi.

Taxi stalls lined the streets outside the arrival areas. They were overflowing with older limousines, newer sedans, Jeepneys, and some vehicles that Ross was not sure were even legal in the United States.

Well, Ross thought, *I'm not in Kansas anymore*.

Almost immediately, taxi drivers pushed, shoved, and jammed in front of him, offering their best fares for anywhere in Manila.

Currently, one Philippine peso was the equivalent of about two cents US, but the American dollar was accepted everywhere, thankfully.

A young driver caught Ross's attention by waving a red handkerchief in front of him. He thumped his chest with his thumb.

"Me sir," said the cabby.

"Who are you?" asked Ross.

"I'm Emanuel."

The young man appeared to be in his late twenties or early thirties. He looked to be full blooded Filipino, with smooth dark skin. Tattered brown leather sandals clung to his feet. His slim waist supported faded blue jeans, which were stylishly ripped across both knees. His lithe shoulders were draped by a white T-shirt on which someone had drawn a six pointed star with a felt tipped marker. His black hair was clean and neatly groomed, shoulder length, and parted in the middle.

The man looked as if he hadn't shaved in a week or two.

He smiled easily and displayed pearly white teeth. His face had a strange glow about it that immediately put Ross at ease. Boyish charm appeared to be his aplomb.

"What are you looking for here?" asked Emanuel.

"I need a ride to my hotel."

"Come," said Emanuel. "Follow me."

Ross picked up his carry-on bag and followed Emanuel to his cab.

It was a Jeepney.

Jeepneys are the Philippines' most popular choice of public transportation. After World War Two, the United States military left hundreds of Willys MB 1/4 ton 4x4 Jeeps in the Philippines for civilian usage. These vehicles were maintained as long as they could be, and when maintenance became impossible, they were torn apart and built and rebuilt over and over again.

This practice has been carried on for decades.

Original military engines were swapped out for anything that could be squeezed under the hoods. Extravagant chrome trimmings and exhaust pipes were installed. Flamboyant multicolored paints were hand brushed on. Hardtops, of every conceivable design, were welded in place.

Perhaps the Jeepneys most endearing feature is the unbelievable number of people that can crowd into one.

Jeepneys have developed into a cultural phenomenon in the Philippines.

Emanuel's Jeepney was no different. It was hand painted a multitude of colors which blended together in a linear patterned mosaic. Perched on its elaborately welded chrome hardtop was a billboard advertisement for a downtown nightclub, named "Heaven on Earth."

Emanuel took Ross's bag and gently placed it into the rear of the Jeepney.

He then ran around to the right side of the vehicle and, beckoning Ross to enter, held open the passenger door.

Bending down and lowering his head, Ross eased his way inside the Jeepney and sat down.

A beautiful aroma of roses immediately overtook Ross.

"Where to sir?" asked Emanuel, glancing at Ross.

"Take me to the Waterfront Pavilion Hotel, please," answered Ross.

Emanuel's face broke into a smile.

"Yes sir, right away sir," beamed Emanuel.

When Ross was in Manila, he always stayed at the Waterfront Pavilion Hotel. Ross found that the hotel's casino provided excellent cover for his clandestine intelligence asset meetings. Not only that, but it was close to the United States Embassy and the Philippine National Bureau of Investigation, to which Ross always required access. It also provided quick and easy egress to the airport and Manila Bay.

One never knew if one would have to leave or escape by land, sea, or air.

The Waterfront Pavilion Hotel is situated on the corner of United Nations Avenue and M.Y. Orosa Street, right between Rizal Park and the UN Avenue train station. The hotel has a rich heritage, and is well known for its warm hospitality. Every room has a computer, with free WIFI internet access.

There were five restaurants to choose from.

Every culinary delight is available, from sweet continental breakfasts, to rich international buffets, to succulent rotisseries.

The cuisine is exquisite.

And most important of all, they have the best French onion soup in Manila.

CHAPTER SEVEN

AVAILABLE

After an engaging demolition derby style race through traffic, the Jeepney pulled up to the front entrance of the Waterfront Pavilion Hotel.

Emanuel scurried out and ran around to the rear of his Jeepney.

He reached in through the open rear window and gently slid out Ross's bag.

Ross opened his passenger door and stepped out stretching.

"Please follow me sir," said Emanuel as he led Ross up the huge concrete steps and through the double glass paned automatic sliding doors into the main lobby.

The lobby of the Waterfront Pavilion Hotel was nothing short of extravagant opulence. A huge crystal chandelier spread its sparkling tentacles three hundred and sixty degrees across the ceiling. The checkered white marble floor flowed out like a vast shimmering ocean from which sprouted towering Grecian pillars supporting the gleaming domed ceiling.

An expanse of curved elaborately hand carved teakwood counters loomed at the approaching pair.

Emanuel walked beside Ross and placed his bag down in front of the first counter from which an overhead placard announced "Concierge" in English.

Ross reached inside his trousers pocket and pulled out a rolled up US twenty dollar bill.

He placed it into Emanuel's hand and said, "Thank you."

Emanuel unfurled the bill and looked at it.

"Thank you, James," said Emanuel.

Ross wondered how this man knew his name.

He probably read it on my luggage tag, he thought.

Emanuel reached into his faded blue jeans pocket and pulled out a business card.

"Here is my card. I also have access to an Albatross seaplane. I can take you deep sea fishing, or SCUBA diving, or just on a tour of the islands. Have you been to our beautiful islands down south?"

"Yes. I've been to some," said Ross. He pondered the offer for a moment.

"How much advance notice time would I have to give you to acquire your services, Emanuel?" asked Ross.

Emanuel's face broadened into a warm smile.

"I'm available. Just call me, day or night. I will come. I can be counted on. I am discreet."

Emanuel continued.

“I am telling you the truth. I can take you anywhere you wish to go.”

Ross gave the business card a quick look and then pocketed it.

“Thanks Emanuel,” said Ross holding out his right hand.

Emanuel’s handshake was warm and firm.

A gentle smile broke out on Emanuel’s face. He turned around and in an instant was gone.

Ross turned his attention to the concierge counter.

The man standing behind the counter appeared to be a native Filipino around forty years of age. His thick black hair was combed straight back and held in place by some type of oily gel. He was impeccably dressed in a dark blue pin-striped three piece suit. His white shirt sported a stiffly starched collar, from which hung a green and white striped tie. The man clasped his hands together in front of him on the counter and eyed Ross up and down.

“Welcome to the Waterfront Pavilion Hotel sir. I am Labbaeus. How may I be of assistance?” asked the Concierge in a very deep baritone voice.

“Well sir, I need a room for at least three nights. I don’t have a reservation,” said Ross reaching in his wallet and pulling out his credit card. “I have stayed here before, however. You should have my credit card on file.”

Ross handed Labbaeus his passport and credit card.

“We are currently booked full sir, but let me see, let me see,” said Labbaeus.

He took Ross’s passport and laid it open on the counter.

Putting on thick reading glasses, Labbaeus began to rapidly type queries into the hotel computer.

In an instant, he found Ross's travel history.

"Yes sir, I see, I see," said Labbaeus. "Ah yes, Mister Ross. You are one of our Gold Line Members. As a courtesy to Gold Line Members, we always keep some rooms in reserve. We just so happen to have a beautiful suite available, sir. Would you like to see it before you choose a selection?"

"I don't have to see it, I'll take it," said Ross gratefully. "The Waterfront's reputation for hospitality is well known and appreciated."

Labbaeus bowed his head saying, "Thank you sir. Thank you indeed sir!"

Labbaeus carefully typed the details into the hotel computer, shifting his gaze between Ross's credit card and the screen.

"There you are sir, you are all set. You'll be staying in room six-two-four. Our porter will assist you."

Labbaeus raised his arm and snapped his fingers.

Immediately, a teenaged male porter shuffled up to Ross.

The porter was wearing white slacks, white shoes, and a white Nehru jacket. The man bowed and reached down picking up Ross's bag.

The porter led Ross to a bank of elevators. He pressed the "UP" button and the elevator doors hissed open. The porter selected the sixth floor button on the control panel and looked at Ross.

"Will you be staying with us long, sir?" inquired the porter.

"No, not really, just a couple of days," said Ross.

The elevator stopped at the sixth floor and the doors slid open.

Ross followed the teenaged porter down the long expanse of plush red carpeted hallway to room 624.

The porter slipped the electronic coded plastic card key into its slot. The small door lock light turned from red to green with an audible *"click."* Pulling the card out, the porter opened the door then gave Ross a tour of the room.

"We have every conceivable amenity available here at the Waterfront, sir," said the porter. "Secure computer access, luxury spas with massage therapy, fully equipped exercise rooms, a magnificent swimming pool, and five delicious restaurants."

"Anything you could possibly need, sir," said the porter smiling.

Ross said, "Thank you," and pressed a ten dollar American bill into the man's hands.

The porter bowed deeply and quickly shuffled out of the room closing the door behind him.

Ross threw his bag on the bed.

He walked over to the room's complimentary Toshiba laptop computer and logged onto the internet.

Ross utilized and accessed the Department of Defense Secret Internet Protocol Router Network to send his emails.

He typed a personal encrypted email to Colonel Gautier:

Sir,
Arrived Manila midnight local time.
Morning resource collection planned.
Updates to follow.
V/r
CPT James B. Ross

That was enough for now, thought Ross.

He pressed the send button and the message was gone through secure SIPRNet channels.

Ross logged off of the Toshiba computer and closed the laptop lid.

He picked up the receiver of the nightstand phone and pressed the wakeup service button.

Ross asked for a wakeup call at five o'clock in the morning.

The soft demure voice of the female receptionist purred, "Certainly sir, have a pleasant evening Mister Ross."

"Thank you, Ma'am," replied Ross.

Ross laid the receiver back in its cradle.

He didn't really need the wakeup call.

Ever since he had attended the Special Forces Qualification Course at Fort Bragg, he could just somehow *will* his body to wake up at anytime. It wasn't magical. It was just something that many SF soldiers were capable of doing.

Noticing a bank of electric outlets on the desk near the phone, Ross plugged his Blackberry cell phone into one for charging.

Next, he opened his suitcase and hung his dark blue suit in the closet, and stowed the rest of his clothes in the draws of the dresser next to the wide screen Sony plasma television.

Ross walked into the bathroom and stripped off his clothes and threw them down.

He loaded his toothbrush with hotel courtesy toothpaste and methodically brushed the staleness of twenty-four hours worth of travel out of his mouth.

Glancing in the mirror and fingering the stubble on his chin, Ross decided to shave in the morning.

He walked over and slid open the twin transparent glass doors of the shower stall and stepped in.

Twisting the crystal power jet handles counterclockwise, he straightened out his arms and leaned forward, pressing both of his palms against the shower wall under the needling spray.

Ross lowered his head and allowed the heavy stream of pulsating hot water to cascade over his aching body.

CHAPTER EIGHT

BETRAYAL

Central Luzon Region Three of the Philippine National Bureau of Investigation was closed at this late hour.

Part of their standard operating procedure was to always have a watch officer manning the phones for any emergencies that would come up after duty hours.

Tonight's watch officer was Special Agent Nestor Lukban.

Special Agent Lukban had the task of monitoring three non-secure, or open, telephone lines.

On these lines anyone could call the Bureau with information pertaining to crimes or leave anonymous tips.

Lukban had reported in a little early for the eleven-to-seven shift.

So far, all he had done was to reroute a call to the Region Seven Office in Cebu.

It's a quiet night, thought Lukban.

I should be grateful.

No sooner had this thought crossed his mind, than phone number two rang, breaking the stillness of the quiet night.

"Hello, this is the National Bureau of Investigations after hours' service officer. How may I help you?" asked Lukban.

Special Agent Lukban held the phone loosely to his left ear and started writing a new entry into the log book in front of him.

"What? Say that again?" a startled Lukban said.

"Who is this please?" asked Lukban.

"How did you come by this information?"

The phone suddenly went dead.

Lukban placed the phone receiver down into its cradle.

He continued entering the call into the log book.

He wrote down everything that had transpired on the anonymous phone call.

Lukban reread his notes and shook his head.

This doesn't make sense, he thought.

An anonymous phone call about an unannounced incursion into sovereign Filipino territory by an American military rescue team?

Why would the Americans do that?

Why would the Americans violate our national sovereignty?

We have good relations with them, don't we?

It doesn't make any sense.

Well, he thought, *I'll give it the attention it's due.*

He signed his name and the time next to the entry on the log sheet.

It is duly noted and will be passed on to the special agent in charge of the day shift.

CHAPTER NINE

SLEEPING SAVIOR

Ross awoke with the jolt of an electric spark.

It was ten minutes before five o'clock in the morning.

As usual, he had mentally impelled himself to wake up through sheer force of will before receiving the hotel's courtesy wakeup telephone call.

Ross staggered into the bathroom, flicking on the lights and fan.

He turned on the shower and stepped in, not wasting any time.

In three minutes his shower was over.

He stepped out of the shower stall and wrapped one of the huge blue terrycloth hotel towels around his waist.

Wiping his right hand across the steam covered mirror, he looked at himself.

He fingered his two mornings' worth of stubble and reached for his AAFES shave gel. With a liberal amount of Army-Air Force Exchange Services shave gel on, he slowly glided his razor across his face. He lowered his head towards the sink and splashed hot water across his face to rinse off the remaining residue. Finally, he poured Aqua Velva aftershave into his cupped left hand and slapped it on his face.

Now he was awake.

Ross walked to the closet and pulled out his dark blue suit.

He dressed quickly.

Highlighting his suit was a white cotton shirt with a narrow black necktie.

Finishing the four-in-hand knot, he cinched up the necktie to his collar.

Ross glanced at himself in the mirror.

I look all right, he thought.

Not too haggard from the flight.

But he had already lost twenty-four hours from travel and a few hours sleeping, and now he had to move quickly.

Ross sat down in front of the courtesy desk in his room and flicked on the ornamental brass reading lamp.

He picked up the landline telephone and placed it squarely in front of him.

Next, he unplugged his charged Blackberry cell phone and scrolled through his contacts.

He found the names and phone numbers of his Philippine assets and started writing them down on a small desktop notepad.

He had twelve local people, which he had used before, for intelligence collection operations.

These were developed intelligence assets, and Ross felt they were all credible and reliable.

He decided that he would try to arrange thirty minute sessions at the hotel's casino, one session per hour.

That was about all the time Ross could afford to give out before trying something else.

I might as well just start at the beginning and go through the list one at a time, thought Ross.

He picked up the receiver and started dialing.

In the snack bar of the Waterfront Pavilion Hotel's casino, Peter Christianson was waiting for his breakfast.

Christianson's breakfast was always the same.

He always ordered scrambled eggs, bacon, hash brown potatoes, white toast with strawberry jam, a large orange juice, and black coffee.

He liked ketchup on his scrambled eggs.

If it was good enough for President Nixon then it's good enough for me, he thought.

He always came here to eat.

That is, he always came here for the last three years.

Today was a celebration.

Today was his birthday.

Today he turned seventy-four years old.

The breakfast came and Christianson stared at it.

He always ordered the same, but his appetite had never been the same.

Nothing had ever been the same since she died.

Nothing had ever been the same since his beloved wife, Judith, passed away three years ago from breast cancer.

Breast cancer, he thought.

How the hell do you get breast cancer?

He realized cancer took many forms and could attack all over the human body, but he always equated cancer with smoking.

Judith had never smoked.

He, on the other hand, had continually smoked a half pack of cigarettes daily since he was eighteen years old in the Marine Corps.

He never got cancer.

He smoked even more since Judith died.

He began drinking more as well.

He had started drinking after Dallas.

But now he drank all the time, as if it could wash away memories, or at least deaden them, dull them.

The doctors told him he would kill himself if he continued with his excessive drinking and smoking.

He asked them how long it would take to die.

Since then he wished for it, even courted it, but it always eluded him, denied him; that elusive demon known as death.

Death.

Peaceful release.

Oblivion.

Painless sleep.

Welcome respite.

Whenever he wished for it, he would remember her.

Oh, how he remembered her!

Judith was a Filipino girl.

They had met when Christianson was stationed at Subic Bay United States Naval Base in 1956.

Judith had silky long black hair, and beautiful smooth skin, with gorgeous sparkling eyes.

She was quiet, and shy, and her smile could light up a room.

He fell in love with her almost immediately, and they were married six months after they first met.

1956.

That was a good year, he thought.

Things seemed so clear, so good, so innocent in 1956.

Christianson had spent two years in the Corps when he married Judith.

They had a simple Catholic wedding in Olongapo City, with all the traditional trimmings of Philippine culture thrown in.

He and Judith had two beautiful daughters, Mary and Elizabeth.

Their life was good, and somehow they survived on the two thousand dollar annual salary a Marine Corps gunnery sergeant made back then.

After his Corps hitch was up, he used the GI Bill to go to the University of Maryland.

Three years later, he graduated with a bachelor degree in criminology and took a chance and applied to the United States Secret Service.

To his surprise, he was accepted.

He had always applied himself to everything he undertook, and the Secret Service job was no different.

Soon he was excelling and found himself, at the age of twenty-five, on the Presidential Protection Detail.

The United States government had found him worthy of trust and confidence to protect President John F. Kennedy.

What a job that was!

Kennedy had exuded charisma and leadership.

But mostly hope.

Hope for the future.

His salary had more than tripled to seven thousand dollars a year, and the future seemed bright.

That is, until Dallas.

November 22nd 1963.

That day changed everything for Christianson.

It changed everything, for the world.

After that nightmare, he slowly began a self destructive descent into madness.

He began drinking heavily.

Severe depression followed.

Could he have sought out help?

Maybe, but he was taught to suppress every emotion.

That's what was expected in the Marine Corps, and then later in the Secret Service.

Be alert.

Be strong.

Take the pain.

Accept it.

Very few sought out psychiatric help back then.

You would have been considered weak.

As the years went on, he masked his addictions with false bravado.

But he was bitter with himself for his own failures, and would not tolerate any mistakes from his children.

So he kept pushing and pushing his daughters to be the best in everything they did.

He would not let up.

Finally, they saw through him and rebelled.

They were all grown up now, with families of their own.

However, Mary and Elizabeth never visited anymore, and his grandchildren were warned of grandpa and his "work hard in school and be the best" speeches.

After the events of Dallas, all he had wanted to do was quit.

But he had a family to support.

Judith and the girls relied on him.

So, he struggled to remain in the Secret Service.

Every day was a grind.

He could not put President Kennedy's assassination behind him.

The least little comment would set him off.

The Warren Commission had made certain recommendations, such as having better communications between government agencies.

But basically the Secret Service had been absolved of blame.

He could not buy that.

He felt he had not been alert enough, which directly led to JFK's death.

He felt responsible for Jacqueline being a widow.

He felt responsible for Caroline and John-John not having a father anymore.

He felt he let the crazies win.

He felt he let the country down.

But he stayed and was placed on other presidential security details.

He worked for LBJ and Nixon, Gerald Ford and Carter.

He had reached twenty years' service right before Reagan was sworn in, so he retired with benefits.

Thank God.

If he had hung around he knew he would have blamed himself for Reagan's shooting as well.

Judith was very supportive of him however.

She constantly told him to ignore the articles he read in the newspapers, about how many shooters there where and from what locations.

She would turn off the television if a story featured purporting to have definitively solved the JFK murder.

She constantly reinforced to him that he had done all anyone could be expected to do.

Judith had urged him to move on with his life; with their life.

Judith was the only reason he had not blown his brains out years ago.

He loved her more than his own life.

So now he was in Manila.

He came back to where he had first met Judith.

He brought her home to be buried in the plot they had purchased over fifty years ago outside of the old Naval Base at Subic Bay.

She was waiting for him.

He wished the wait would not be too much longer.

Peter Christianson stared back at his breakfast.

He picked at the eggs and ate the bacon.

Then he downed the orange juice and started sipping the coffee.

He looked around and motioned for the waiter to come over.

He ordered a Bloody Mary to be brought to him on the casino floor.

Not too early for a drink, he thought.

He paid his bill and walked out of the snack bar and into the casino.

Looking around, he selected a small cocktail table where he could observe the casino action and settled down to enjoy his drink.

It was his first drink of the day.

And the drinks kept coming.

PART TWO

Nothing exceeds the vanity of our existence but the folly of our pursuits.

Oliver Goldsmith
1728 — 1774
Irish Playwright

CHAPTER TEN

CLOSE YOUR EYES AND SEE

If there was one thing Peter Christianson was good at, it was summing up people.

He learned that technique back in his days with the Secret Service.

He learned how to immediately determine if someone posed a threat or not.

For several hours now, he had been observing a young man in the casino conducting what appeared to be interviews.

But there was something different about these interviews and this young man.

The young man was sitting in a wicker chair at a cocktail table, dressed in a dark blue suit with white shirt and black necktie. His hair was short and he looked extremely fit. The way he walked and carried himself displayed an air of authority, and something else.

Christianson couldn't quite put his finger on it.

Yes, of course, he thought.

This young man exuded what could only be described as an air of controlled violence.

He had witnessed that before, in the Marine Corps.

Hour after hour, Christianson watched as this young man waited for, and talked to, an assorted cast of characters.

Christianson watched.

He watched the young man greet his hosts and beckon them to chair.

Some of the interviewees were young men in suits who could pass as businessmen. Some were smartly attired professional looking women. Others looked like punks who came off the street corner somewhere. The one thing they all had in common was courtesy and a look of determination on their faces.

He watched as the young man carefully asked questions and diligently wrote notes down on a small pad in front of him.

Always there was the handshake, and the forced smile.

This went on and on.

Lunch came and went.

The interviews continued.

Maybe this guy is interviewing folks for a hotel job?

No, can't be.

He doesn't fit the profile, thought Christianson.

This guy is too stoical, too controlled, like a capped volcano waiting.

Dinner time came.

Christianson was getting ready to order, when he noticed the young man perform a peculiar ritual.

The young man had been sitting alone for several minutes now, and it appeared as if the interviews were over. He displayed a look of exasperation on his face, and suddenly threw his pen down on the table. The young man then abruptly, methodically, folded the piece of paper he had been writing on length wise, over and over on top of itself. Then, he expanded it, and placed the accordion folded paper standing upright inside an ashtray. Next, the young man lit a match and touched it on each side of the top of the paper, allowing it to burn down at the same controlled rate. When there were only ashes left, he placed his drink glass over them and twisted and turned it, extinguishing and mixing the ashes.

The interviews were definitely over.

This guy is an intelligence agent, thought Christianson.

He had just witnessed a typical example of classic intelligence tradecraft in action.

Something was nagging at Christianson; an inner, unexplainable urging.

He looked at his bar tab and paid it, counting out crisp US dollars.

Leaning forward to compensate for his arthritic knees, Christianson used his arms and pushed himself up and out of his chair.

He had made his decision.

I better approach this young man from the front, thought Christianson.

Ross noticed a man walking deliberately towards him, coming closer and closer.

He noticed the gray hair.

This guy is elderly.

At least seventy years old, thought Ross.

The old man was dressed in a black suit, with a white shirt and narrow black necktie.

As he got closer, Ross noticed the black wingtip shoes on his feet.

Old school, thought Ross.

The old man looks like a mortician, Ross further mused.

Christianson stopped in front of Ross's table and said, "Excuse me young man, may I join you?"

Ross stood up politely and offered a chair.

He could smell the alcohol on the old man.

"Please do," said Ross.

Ross stretched out his right arm and offered his hand.

The old man grasped it in a firm handshake.

Christianson pulled out a wicker chair and sat down at Ross's small casino cocktail table.

Ross stared at the old man, observing every detail.

His thinning gray hair was actually white. There was the beginning of a bald spot on the crown. His eyes were bloodshot, yet brilliantly blue-gray. He had high cheek bones, and his face was still handsome, though badly weathered by time and probably stress.

This guy had to be in his seventies.

His skin was pale and looked starched, like the white shirt he was wearing. His suit coat, pants, wingtip shoes, and narrow necktie, were all black in color.

The guy had some kind of wide golden colored tie clip holding his necktie in place.

It resembled a boat of some sort.

"Can I get you a drink, sir?" asked Ross.

Christianson thought a moment.

Something had brought him to this table.

Something had seated him next to this young man.

He wasn't here to drink, or chat, or dwindle away the time.

Something was nagging at him about this young man.

Something was nagging at him about himself.

He needed a mission.

He needed to do *something*, *anything* that was worthwhile and could help someone.

He had nothing else.

He had wished for death for so long that he was tired.

Now, he wanted to help someone, anyone.

He could tell that this young guy needed his help.

Christianson closed his eyes and saw.

He closed his eyes and saw hauntingly vivid images of his daughters, of Judith, and of Dallas.

"Coffee will be fine," said Christianson as he opened his eyes.

Ross caught the attention of a waiter and held up two fingers saying, "Two Barako coffees please, sir."

Ross turned his attention to the old man.

He could see the tie clip better now.

The old man was wearing, what appeared to be, a golden World War Two PT boat tie clip.

On the bow of the PT boat was engraved the number 109.

That was the number of President John F. Kennedy's old US Navy Patrol Torpedo boat, thought Ross.

He had read the stories of JFK distributing those tie clips as gifts to his friends and staff during his administration.

That was nearly fifty years ago.

“So what brings you here, sir? Gambling?” asked Ross.

“No, I’m not gambling. Please excuse my bad manners. My name is Peter Christianson. I’ve noticed you for some time now. You look like you’re frustrated. You look like you could use some help with something.”

Ross replied, “My name is James Ross. No, I’m just trying to get some information in order to make a decision, that’s all.”

The coffee came.

Christianson leaned forward and picked up his cup.

“So what is this Barako coffee, anyway?” asked Christianson.

Ross smiled.

“It’s from the Batangas Provence in southwest Luzon, originally made from plants imported from Brazil in the 1800s. It has a strong taste and is well known as an antioxidant.”

Christianson took a sip and smiled. “It’s good, very good.”

He looked at Ross and decided to cash in all his chips.

“Now listen son, I’m going to cut to the chase. I know you are in intelligence,” said Christianson revealingly. “I saw the way you destroyed your notes. They don’t teach that at Princeton. I’m retired US government myself. Maybe I can help you. I’ve lived here for years. You could say I grew up here.”

Christianson paused, and then continued.

“If you are in intelligence, then you are here about terrorism. If you are here about terrorism, then you must be interested in the most recent developments, and that means, to me, you must be here about the recent kidnapping of the CIA guy.”

Ross was startled and intrigued.

Needing time to think, Ross decided to change the subject.

Handing Christianson a menu, Ross said, "Have you eaten dinner, sir? Would you care to join me?"

Ross's mind was swirling with what Christianson had just told him, but he forced himself to turn around and look for a waitress.

Ross raised his right hand and caught the attention of a pretty Philippine waitress.

She scurried over and stood, with pen and pad in hand, eagerly waiting to write down their order.

All of eighteen years old, the waitress was very beautiful with jet black hair, which cascaded around her face with tiny curls, and hung low caressing the high button-on-the-side white collar which stood alone accenting her luxurious neck. Her black blouse was draped low, elegantly revealing soft shoulders and bosom, and the little black skirt was stretched taunt across her buttocks. The whole outfit was tied together with a three inch wide white belt with large silver buckle. Five inch stiletto heeled matching black shoes with open toes topped off the ensemble. Her fingernails were cut close and painted white, and she wore no stockings.

She didn't have to.

As with all Asian women, her legs were naturally silky smooth and never required shaving.

She smelled of Florecita eau de parfum.

A plastic name tag pinned above her left breast proudly proclaimed her name to be "Maggie."

Ross said, "I'll have the Bistek Tagalog sirloin beef strips, slowly cooked in soy sauce, with calamansi juice and onions. Bring some lumpia spring rolls, a small bowl of patis fish sauce, and some biskotso bread with coconut jam."

Writing it down, Maggie asked, "Anything else, sir?"

"Yes, bring a bottle of banana ketchup please. I love that stuff," said Ross looking at Christianson.

Maggie further asked, "And for your salad, sir?"

"A garden salad with Thousand Island dressing, please," replied Ross.

"And to drink sir?" asked Maggie.

"Let me have unsweetened iced tea, please," answered Ross.

Ross had asked the next question at dozens of restaurants throughout Southeast Asia. He enjoyed the routine and loved the responses. Mostly though, he loved the soup.

"Do you have French onion soup today?" inquired Ross.

Maggie looked up from her notepad and smiled.

"Why yes sir. The best French onion soup in the whole Philippines," she said proudly.

"Okay. I'll have the French onion soup, with a large thin slice of cheese melted over the top," said Ross returning her smile.

Maggie smiled back and looked at Christianson.

"Well, that all sounds unbelievably good. I'll have the same please," said Christianson.

"French onion soup too, sir?" asked Maggie.

Christianson looked at Ross and closed his menu.

"Yes, I don't think I can pass that up," he said grinning.

Ross gathered the menus and handed them to Maggie.

She smiled and walked away.

The scent of her perfume lingered.

Both men sipped their coffee while their eyes followed Maggie's departure.

Setting his coffee cup down on the table, Christianson decided to break the ice.

Reaching into his front left suit coat pocket, Christianson pulled out an old, worn out, black leather wallet.

He slid it across the small table to Ross.

Ross lifted the wallet and flipped it open.

Inside the wallet, staring at Ross was the five pointed gold star and credentials establishing Peter Christianson to be a United States Secret Service Agent.

Across the face of this Department of the Treasury official credential was punched out, in barely visible tiny pin pricks, letters that spelled the word R-E-T-I-R-E-D.

Ross held the credentials and stared at them.

They were dated 1960.

These were issued when the Secret Service was still under the Treasury Department.

About ten years ago, their jurisdictional status changed to fall under the Department of Homeland Security.

Ross closed the wallet and slid it back across the table to Christianson.

"What's on your mind, sir?" asked Ross.

Christianson replied, "First of all, please call me Peter, and not *Sir.*"

"Okay, Peter," said Ross.

Christianson continued.

"You look like whatever information you were trying to get from those twelve people you interviewed did not pan out. You have a frustrated look on your face."

"Listen, son. Let me help you. I have nothing else to do."

"Let me help you out."

"The kidnapping of that CIA guy named Kloet is all over the newspapers. You're trying to get information on that, I figure."

"Hell, even my waiter told me three hours ago that's what you were doing."

"Everyone here knows."

"You can't keep something like that a secret in a Manila casino nowadays."

Ross smiled.

"Well, Peter, that's interesting," said Ross. "And you're right. I'm in the Army, and that's what I'm doing. I'm trying to get information to find out where exactly Mister Kloet is being held."

Christianson finished the sentence for him.

"To mount a rescue operation, right?" said Christianson.

"Well," said Ross, "something like that. I've got one more lead, one more interview to conduct. I got referred to another asset who may be able to provide some current information on Kloet's whereabouts."

Ross did not tell him that he had struck out miserably with the other twelve informants.

Maggie, the waitress, approached their small table, interrupting the conversation.

"Here you go, sirs," said Maggie. She placed their sizzling plates in front of them, including the hot bowls of French onion soup.

Ross and Christianson temporarily postponed their conversation to begin eating.

As Christianson sampled the soup, he said, "This French onion soup is really delicious. The melted cheese really highlights the flavor."

With a mouthful of food, Ross said, "I know, I order it here all the time."

Ross continued munching his food and thinking to himself.

Why not use the old man's experience?

I've pulled a blank with my original informants.

No one wants to talk for fear of Abu Sayyaf retribution.

Time is running short and I've got nothing to lose.

Maybe he can help me.

Maybe he does know this country better than me.

Maybe Peter Christianson is just the miracle I need.

Ross said, "As I was saying, there's one more asset coming to talk to me, a Mister Basil Voorschott. He should be here about the time we finish with dinner."

"If you don't mind then Jim, just let me sit here with you. I'll just listen. I used to conduct interviews before, hundreds of them. Maybe when it's over, I can offer you some advice. Maybe I'll hear something you didn't," said Christianson.

"I hope so, Peter," said Ross. "Right now I can use all the help I can get."

Ross decided to change the subject.

"Tell me, what was it like working for JFK?"

Christianson looked surprised.

"How do you know that? How do you know I worked for him?" asked Christianson.

"Well I'm just assuming, but I'd guess you did from the PT 109 tie clip you're wearing."

Christianson smiled and, looking down, ran his fingers across his ancient cherished tie clip.

"He gave them to us you know," said Christianson. "He gave them to all of his protection detail."

Then he looked down at his plate.

He allowed himself to drift back in time and space; back to another era; an era of grace and innocence, vigor and compassion, progress and substance, fear and hope. His mind clouded, and then became clear and crisp with vivid details about President Kennedy; his smile, his warmth, his jovial nature, his intelligence, and his friendship.

"That was the best job I ever had, and the worst. I can't speak for anyone else on the detail, but I enjoyed every day with the Boss. He was very personable and seemed to care about people. At least that's the impression he gave you. But I think it was sincere. I think he was sincere and truly wanted a better world."

"I wish I could give him my badge and tell him how much I miss him."

Christianson put down his spoon and looked at Ross's face.

"I was in Dallas when it happened. I was part of the motorcade security detail. We always knew something could happen at any time. We trained constantly for it. But it was just unbelievable when it did. It was so quick."

Christianson's eyes drifted to some spot above and to the left of Ross's head and just stared.

He began talking in a monotone about events that he had replayed a thousand times over and over again in his mind.

“Looking back at it, I’m sure I did all I could have. At least that’s what everybody told me. Everybody said we did all we could have done,” said Christianson in a robotic automatic resonance.

“But others — some others — wanted our heads. They wrote report after report saying we were inept and unfit for protective security. Some said we lacked leadership, that we had no clue how to interact with and protect a robust President. Some wanted us to be punished and lose our jobs. Some wanted us taken off of protection and put on administrative duties.”

Now his gaze focused back into Ross’s eyes with a sudden melancholy sadness.

“But I never paid attention to those critics. All I knew was that the man was dead. The Boss was dead and we failed him.”

“I could have done more. I know it. The man was gunned down in broad daylight and I watched. The man I was sworn to protect. Sure, anyone can take a shot at anyone. But we should have cancelled the damned motorcade from the get go. We should have cancelled when we first got the reports of the nut-jobs in Dallas.”

“I don’t know why we didn’t cancel that motorcade.”

“We could have made the President understand.”

“I’m sure we could have made him understand.”

“We could have made him understand.”

Ross was silent.

He was witnessing a shattered man.

Christianson said, “You know, you never really get over anything like that. Hell, there never was anything like that. You learn to live with stuff, with outcomes, but you never truly get over them.”

"There is no closure. No sir. There is no such thing as closure. You just have to lock it away in your mind. You have to suppress it. You have to block it out so you can continue with your mission."

"That's what we did. That's what I did."

"We didn't have any therapy. We didn't have any stress response teams to help us, like they have today. I think that stuff would have been useful though."

"But back then, we didn't have the time. We had another President to protect. Hell, for all we knew it could have been an international conspiracy and LBJ would have been next."

"So, we just pushed on."

Christianson's sad eyes pleaded with Ross.

"I really want to help you Jim, anyway I can. Your buddy, Kloet, deserves to be saved. All this damn terrorism needs to stop. It needs to be ended. These damn radicals need to be put away. We can't let this continue in the world. One day, your kids will want to go to college and get a job, and they deserve a safe world to do it in."

"I know I can help you. I'm not so physically fit anymore, but I can keep up, you won't have to worry. And I've got decades of experience that may come in useful."

Ross listened and nodded his head slowly up and down in understanding.

Then both men turned and continued finishing their dinners.

CHAPTER ELEVEN

DECISION TIME

Maggie the waitress could see that Ross and Christianson were finished eating.

She walked to the table and asked, "Any dessert for you gentlemen?"

Ross looked at Christianson who shook his head negatively.

"Nope Maggie, that will be all. It was all very delicious," said Ross.

He looked at the check and paid it with forty US dollars, and then handed Maggie a ten dollar tip.

"Thank you Maggie, for such great service," said Ross.

Maggie smiled. "Thank you sir, and please come again."

Ross looked at his Benrus wristwatch.

Its luminescent hands displayed eight o'clock in the evening.

Ross said, "This Mister Voorschott should be coming along at any moment."

Christianson looked around and adjusted his seat so he was sitting closer to Ross.

Both men sipped their after dinner Barako coffees.

After about fifteen minutes, a man entered the casino from the south side and headed towards Ross's table.

Ross and Christianson watched the man approach.

The man was tall for a Filipino, at least five foot eleven inches. His short gray hair was well groomed and combed to the right side. He had a neatly trimmed silver-gray mustache which gave him a roguish look. His skin was darkly tanned with a leathery appearance from years in the sun. His eyes were black and highlighted with thin, black brows. He was wearing a white two piece suit, with silk white shirt, and a bright red necktie.

His face looked angular, lean, and hard.

He was wearing a gold ring displaying a large red ruby in it on the third finger of his left hand. He looked like he weighed around one hundred and seventy-five pounds. It was hard to determine how old he was, probably late sixties or early seventies.

The man looked like he meant business.

Approaching Ross's table, the man's face broke into a huge smile.

"Excuse me sirs, I am looking for a Mister Ross. Would either one of you gentlemen happen to be him?" asked the tall dark Filipino man bowing over at the waist.

Ross rose up from the table.

"Yes sir, I'm Ross. This is Mister Christianson. You must be Mister Basil Voorschott then?" inquired Ross.

"At your service, Mister Ross," said Voorschott straightening up. "Here is my identification."

Voorschott handed Ross his Philippine driver's license.

"Please sit down sir," said Ross.

Voorschott sat down in the wicker chair opposite Ross. He crossed his right leg over his left knee and observed Ross examining his license.

Ross looked at the driver's license. He jotted down the license number and a few notes on a fresh piece of notepad paper. Then he handed the driver's license back to Voorschott and leaned forward in his chair.

Before he could ask another question, Voorschott spoke.

"So, Mister Ross, I understand you are looking for the American, this Mister Kloet," said Voorschott.

Voorschott reached inside his suit coat pocket and pulled out a slim silver cigarette case. Clicking it open, he extracted a thin dark brown cigarette which he placed between his dried out lips.

A stick match appeared between the fingers of his left hand which he lit by striking across the top of his left thumb.

After lighting his cigarette, Voorschott observed the match flame for several seconds and then extinguished the match by pressing it between his left hand thumb and forefinger.

He threw the lifeless match into the tabletop crystal astray and let out a hiss of tobacco vapors through his nostrils.

Ross and Christianson were mesmerized by the cigarette lighting ceremony.

"Why do you seek this man?" asked Voorschott.

"Well, to negotiate his release," said Ross.

"I see, I see," said Voorschott.

"Well then, you are in luck. I have found out, through my own contacts, that this man, Kloet, is being held on Jolo Island in Sulu Province. He is in Jolo City in an Abu Sayyaf safe house, if you want to call it that."

Ross and Christianson looked at each other and then back at Voorschott.

"What do you mean?" asked Ross.

"It looks more like a shack to me," said Voorschott.

Voorschott continued.

"I have the address as well," he said.

"Tell me, is this Kloet a friend of yours, Mister Ross? Do you personally know him?"

"He's a colleague, sir," answered Ross.

"Ah yes, yes, very well. I can help you then," said Voorschott.

"I know how precious a brother's blood is."

Then Voorschott began a strange homily.

"Mister Ross, what can I offer you? What can I offer anyone? If I had a wife, I could offer her love. If I had children, I could offer them a future. But I have none of these, Mister Ross. My existence is like the rays of the sun. All the rays lead back to me, only me."

Ross and Christianson became mystified by Voorschott's sudden cryptic sermon.

Voorschott continued, "But I do have something to offer you, Mister Ross, from the simple fact that you are here asking me about this man. I can tell that you are a man of principle. I can tell that you mean what you say. I will give you the information you seek."

Ross relaxed back in his chair, not sure where this conversation was going.

Voorschott said, "But I also am a man of principle. I will give you the information, and I only ask for one thing in return."

Ross leaned forward again.

He had to trust Voorschott.

He had not one other shred of valid information to move on.

There were only forty-eight hours left before Kloet was to be killed.

Time was desperately running out.

"What do you want in return sir?" asked Ross.

Voorschott looked at both Ross and Christianson.

"You see, gentlemen, I am a patriot."

"Let me explain further."

"My mother was Dutch and worked for the Red Cross here before World War Two. She met my father, who was full blooded Filipino, and working in a small but prosperous jewelry store in Manila. They were married and had a fine life together."

"Then the War started and the Imperial Japanese Army invaded."

"Well, my father's store was ransacked and closed down. So, my father joined the Filipino guerrillas, the underground. He fought alongside the American forces all over Luzon. But the Imperial Japanese Army proved to be too much for them, and he was captured at Bataan."

Voorschott paused, and his eyes glazed over.

"My father was horribly tortured."

"He died on the Bataan Death March."

"My mother changed my last name to her maiden name to provide safety for me."

Ross looked at Christianson.

Voorschott said, “I loved my father. My mother raised me and somehow we survived the war. Today, I am a successful businessman, but I never forgot what evil did to my father. I hate all forms of evil, whether it’s imperialism, fascism, communism, or terrorism, whatever.”

“I hate it all.”

“Therefore, I will be glad to give you the information you need.”

“The only thing I request, the only thing I want you to do is …”

Ross and Christianson clung to Voorschott’s every word.

“All I want is for you to tell Mister Kloet that the son of a Filipino hero gave you the information to save him.”

Ross said smiling, “I absolutely will guarantee that, sir.”

“Very Good, Mister Ross,” said Voorschott. “Then it is settled. And thank you.”

Ross picked up his pen and steadied his notepad on his knees.

Voorschott said, “Mister Kloet is being held in a house, a shack really, at number five-seventeen Bata-Bata Road.”

“It is easy to access.”

“Once you get to Jolo City, take Sawaki Boulevard to Bayog Road, and then you will see Bata-Bata. Follow it to number five-seventeen.”

“There may be two to three men guarding him. They appear to be home grown Aby Sayyaf men from Jolo.”

“It’s such a shame that some young Filipino men have been sucked into that cesspool known as Abu Sayyaf.”

“They are just thugs really.”

“Anyway, that is the information I have.”

Ross wrote it all down.

Then he took the sheet of paper and tore around the part with the address on it, making it into a smaller piece, and folded it and shoved it into his trousers pocket.

Christianson stared at Voorschott. He knew there was more coming.

"Oh, there is one more thing gentlemen," said Voorschott.

"There have been rumors that an American was seen with Kloet several times. The American is a white male, six feet tall, forty or so years old, around two hundred pounds, with short brown hair and a goatee."

Ross looked up from his notepad.

"I have ascertained that the American is a professional of some sort. At least he dresses well, like a professional should."

"Exactly what he does or who he is, no one knows."

"However, he has been seen outside the shack, and also viewed going inside. And this shack is small. Not more than, perhaps six hundred square feet, with a palm thatched roof and bamboo sides."

Ross wrote it all down.

"Well, that's really all I have for you, Mister Ross," said Voorschott. "As I said, I am a patriot first and foremost. I hope you can finesse Mister Kloet's release. And I hope those who caused this incident pay, and that their faces are erased from my beloved Philippines forever."

Voorschott looked at both Ross and Christian, and then stood up and thrust out his right hand.

"Here is my business card with my personal cell number and email address. Call me if you need anything else, anything at all," said Voorschott.

Ross and Christian stood up simultaneously.

Ross took the card and shook Voorschott's hand.

"Thank you sir. This means a lot to me," said Ross.

Voorschott shook hands with Christianson and said, "It was a pleasure to meet you sir."

"Likewise," said Christianson.

"Well then, good evening gentlemen," said Voorschott.

Voorschott turned around and walked away from the cocktail table and out of the casino.

Still standing, Ross said to Christianson, "Listen Peter, I'm going to accept your offer, if it's still on the table?"

Christianson beamed, "It sure is Jim. It sure is."

"But we've got to move quickly because there isn't much time left," Ross said.

"Kloet is to be killed in two days. We need to get to Jolo Island and fast, and I know just the person to take us there."

Ross reached into his suit coat pocket and pulled out Emanuel's business card. He punched the number into his Blackberry cell phone and waited.

After four rings, someone answered.

"Hello?"

Ross replied, "Yes hello. I'm trying to find Emanuel. Is he around?"

"This is Emanuel. How can I help you?"

"This is James Ross. You drove me from the airport to the Waterfront Pavilion Hotel yesterday. Do you remember?"

Emanuel replied, "Why yes, Mister Ross. I do remember. James Ross, right? I am with another fare right now, but how can I be of service to you?"

"Emanuel, I need to employ your services to go down south for a trip. I and a friend of mine need to get to Jolo Island as soon as possible. When can we leave?" asked Ross, "the sooner the better."

Emanuel said, "Well sir, I always keep my Albatross fueled and ready to go for just such a situation. I moor it in the bay, at a place just around the corner from the Manila Yacht Club. It's at pier number six, dock space number one. That pier is a really long one that extends out into the bay, and I'm at the end of it. You can't miss it. And don't worry, I keep it stocked with everything a gentleman may require, refreshments, food, fishing supplies, and diving gear."

"Okay," said Ross. "And what if we were going to do some hunting on Jolo?"

"Hunting?" asked Emanuel searchingly.

"Yes," replied Ross looking at Christianson, "hunting."

Emanuel said, "What kind of hunting? I mean, what kind of equipment would you need?"

"Well, we would need some long range rifles, for wild boar of course, and some pistols to finish the job when we got up close," said Ross.

There was silence on Emanuel's end of the phone for a few seconds. Then he spoke.

"Well, let me see what I can do. I'll definitely get you what I can Mister Ross," said Emanuel.

Ross looked at Christianson and both men smiled.

"Okay, that'll be fine then. We need a little time to change and get ready."

Ross glanced at his battered Benrus watch.

Its luminous hands displayed nine o'clock in the evening.

"We'll meet you in, say, one hour at your plane. I guess there can't be too many Grumman Albatross planes docked at Manila Bay, right?" asked Ross.

"No there are not. I am the only one sir, and I will be waiting for you and your friend," said Emanuel.

Ross answered, "Okay, that'll be fine. See you Emanuel."

"Wait a minute sir, hold on for a second. I know you aren't going to believe this, but the passenger I have in the back of my taxi says she knows you. I picked her up from the airport just ten minutes ago, and when she heard me say your name just now on the phone, she screamed so loud I thought my ears would burst. She wants to talk to you. Here you go."

Emanuel passed his cell phone over to the young lady in the back of his taxi.

"Hello?" said Ross.

"My God James, I can't believe it's you!" gasped Lin.

Ross's heart skipped a beat.

The young lady was Lin Sparrow.

He recognized Lin's voice immediately, and a dozen emotions swept over him.

"Lin? What are you doing here?"

"I'm here to find you and warn you of the terrible dreams and premonitions I've been having of you," said Lin, cupping her hand around the cell phone and lowering her voice to a whisper.

"I feel your life is in danger. I think Creedmoor is trying to — to kill you. He's plotting something. He's in all of my nightmares. Oh James, James! It's just horrible! I had to come to find you and warn you, don't you see?"

Ross's thoughts were swirling.

"All right Lin, all right, just stay with Emanuel the taxi driver. We're meeting him at his plane. I can't talk now, but I'll explain everything when I see you," said Ross, his mind racing.

"My God it's a miracle I found you James. Okay. I'll be there as soon as I can."

"Okay Lin, see you then."

"See you soon James."

Lin handed the cell phone back to Emanuel.

Emanuel said, "Well it certainly is an interesting world, isn't it sir?"

"Unbelievable Emanuel," said Ross, truly stunned.

"Well, I'd better go now. Yes sir, we'll see you soon." With that, Emanuel ended the call, and placed his cell phone on the seat next to him. He started smiling.

Ross pressed the power end button once on his Blackberry cell phone and hung up. He put the Blackberry inside his trousers pocket. His head was spinning with the thought of Lin Sparrow being here.

Lin Sparrow.

The Malaysian woman he had met last summer.

She was the girl who had changed his life for the better.

She was the lady he couldn't stop thinking about.

Ross looked at Christianson and said, "Well Peter, we have an additional asset now to help us."

"Who might that be?" inquired Christianson.

"My friend. It's a long story, and I'll tell you when this is all over, okay?"

"Sure, no problem. I'm just glad you're letting me help you out. So, who is this guy Lin we're meeting anyway? Is he another intelligence type, or maybe one of your Army buddies?"

"No, not really. Lin is actually a she. Lin's a member of the United States Department of State from Malaysia."

"Oh, I see," said Christianson pondering the possibilities.

"Lin has a certain set of skills that come in useful at times. Have you ever heard of the United States Army Operational Group at Fort Meade Maryland, and the Remote Viewing Project?"

Christianson scratched his head. "Yeah, I think I saw a History Channel story on that unit awhile back. Isn't that the one with clairvoyance and all that dreaming and mind telepathy stuff?"

"That's it. Well, Lin Sparrow is right up there with the best of those guys," said Ross.

"But Lin is also a registered nurse. Those medical skills always come in handy."

"Listen Peter, I told Emanuel we would meet him in one hour at his plane, so, whatever you need to do, go ahead and do it. My room is upstairs, so I can change quickly out of this suit, how about you?"

Christianson looked at Ross and thought a moment.

He said, "Okay Jim, do whatever you need to. I'll meet you right here, whenever you're ready. I'm staying with my brother-in-law over in Olongapo City these days. But I don't need to get anything there. I'm ready as I am, right now."

Ross looked at Christianson: at the black suit, necktie, wingtips, and white shirt; and suddenly had a surging sense of pride pour over him. It pricked the small hairs on the nape of his neck and made his cheeks flush.

The guy is professional, thought Ross. *He was actually in his Secret Service uniform: black suit and necktie, white shirt and black wingtip shoes. That's how this guy operated. He didn't need anything to go into action.*

Ross looked at his Benrus again.

"There is only a little over forty-eight hours left for us to reach Kloet, and I guess I can't let you be the only one *stylishly* attired. Emanuel sure is going to wonder what the hell is going on the way we're dressed, but so what, let's go," Ross said with determined finality.

Christianson nodded his head in acknowledgement to Ross.

Both men, walking side by side, sauntered out of the casino, and into the foreboding of the dark Manila evening.

It was the typhoon season, and the tropical monsoon rains were already being pulled in across the archipelago. The rains were coming down hard and drenching everything in sight.

Ross looked around and immediately hailed a taxi.

The taxicab spun around the pick-up/drop-off circle in front of the glittering casino entrance. Screeching to a halt in front of them, the driver scurried out through the torrential downpour and opened the right rear passenger door as both men ducked inside.

Huddled together in the backseat of the cab, dripping wet, each man anticipated in his own mind what fate awaited them.

CHAPTER TWELVE

TRAITOR

Nine hundred and fifty-two kilometers away, on Jolo Island, Randal Kloet was running over escape and evasion options in his mind.

The anesthetized feeling had left him, but he noticed he still had the intravenous plastic tubing running from his left arm to the bag hanging on the stainless steel hospital pole next to him.

He could clearly read the words *VECURONIUM BROMIDE* stamped across the center of the plastic bag.

What these words meant, he could only surmise.

Kloet figured it was some sort of paralytic agent.

The solution must be clearly turned off now, or at a reduced dosage, he thought, as he could now feel all his limbs move when he willed it.

That did not change his situation, however.

Three Filipino men were in the room, pointing AK-47 rifles at him. The men were young, each around eighteen or nineteen years old. They were dressed in colorful T-shirts, blue jeans, and had sandals on their feet. They were thin, and gave off the appearance of being street punks, or thugs. The men each sat on small bamboo chairs, about four meters in front of Kloet.

The room was the same one he had originally woke up in: thatched palm roof, bamboo walls, and dirt floor. The metal framed twin bed he had been lying on was next to him, to the right. But now, he was sitting in a rickety bamboo chair, with a small table in front of him fashioned out of driftwood.

There was a bowl of rice and baked beans on the table, and a plastic bottle of water.

Kloet was famished.

He picked up the bowl and scooped rice and beans with his right hand, shoveling it into his mouth.

Next, he unscrewed the top off the bottle and guzzled water down his throat.

The guards began to smile at one another, at Kloet's seeming desperation.

It was night outside, and the shack was lit by a solitary light bulb dangling from the ceiling.

Kloet could hear the monsoon rains pelting the exterior.

Suddenly, the front door of the shack was flung open, allowing the rains to slosh in and causing the solitary light fixture to sway back and forth, splashing illumination off the walls.

Through the doorway downpour stepped a man.

The man was tall, six feet at least. He was in his early forties, and looked like he weighed a very fit two hundred pounds. His hair was dark brown and combed straight back. The man's chin sported a well-kept goatee.

He was wearing a short sleeved, brightly colored, floral designed island shirt. Khaki pants hung at his hips. His feet were nestled in US Army issued, steel soled, black leather jungle boots, with the olive drab green canvas sides.

On his wrist was a stainless steel Omega Seamaster chronometer watch.

His dark eyes seemed to dart around and capture everything in the room.

The man was soaking wet from head to toe, and, upon entering, wiped the rain off his forehead with a swipe of his right hand, flicking the droplets to the dirt floor.

Kloet could not believe his eyes.

It was Julius Creedmoor!

Creedmoor was the rogue CIA Case Officer who had sold his soul to the international terrorist group known as Abu Sayyaf, and had betrayed Kloet and his friend, James Ross, nearly three months ago in Malaysia. He was believed to have been shot dead, or at least drowned, in the Sungai Gombak River in Kuala Lumpur.

What the hell was Creedmoor doing here?

Kloet got his answer quickly.

"God damn it's wet out there," said Creedmoor, stomping his feet as he entered.

He turned around and shut the door behind him, sliding closed the deadbolt.

Nodding hello to the three Abu Sayyaf agents, Creedmoor snatched up a bamboo chair from the corner of the room, and pulled it around so he was sitting directly across the table from Kloet.

"Hello Randal," said Creedmoor looking around. "Please forgive these less than stalwart accommodations."

Kloet stared at Creedmoor incredulously.

"I'm glad to see you survived your ordeal, more or less intact. For whatever its worth, the young lady who drugged you was," Creedmoor searched for the proper words, "reluctant to do so. I just thought you'd like to know that."

Kloet took another drink from his water bottle.

"It's always been curious to me, how these bargirls seem to have such a big heart and real emotional affection," said Creedmoor.

"I think it goes to show, that you don't appreciate anything when you are born with everything, and that those who are born with nothing appreciate everything more. Don't you agree, Randal?"

Creedmoor waited for Kloet to respond.

Kloet said nothing.

"I suppose you must have a million questions about what's going on and what this is all about?" asked Creedmoor.

"Well, as easily as you were caught, you certainly don't belong in the Agency as a Case Officer. I hear they may have an opening for a man of your caliber over in the Keystone Cops however. You really are second string, Randal."

Kloet realized Creedmoor was trying to bait him now, trying to make him lose his cool.

He struggled to maintain his composure.

"What do you want Creedmoor? Is this about ransom? What are you after? What is this all about?" asked Kloet.

"What this is all about....as you so eloquently put it....is me."

Creedmoor stood up and began to pace around the room.

"After that disagreeable episode in Malaysia, I have become a hunted man. I am hunted by the State Department, the Central Intelligence Agency, Interpol, and just about every other international police organization you care to mention. I am hunted because of you and your friend Ross."

Kloet decided to engage the conversation, to stir things up a bit.

"You're hunted because you're a traitor who sold out his country, Julius."

Creedmoor stopped pacing in mid stride and turned around to look at Kloet.

"Is that the extent of your vision, Randal? Is that really all you see? What do you know? You don't really know anything about me. I've been employed by the Central Intelligence Agency for over ..."

Kloet cut him off.

"You *were* employed by the Central Intelligence Agency," said Kloet.

"Okay, fine. I'll give you that. I *was* employed by the Central Intelligence Agency for over twenty-two years."

"And what did it get me?"

"It got me two divorces and two ex-wives fighting over what little money I earned. I traveled around the world so much I barely got to know either of them. But that's what you get for volunteering for every hardship assignment there is in the hopes that your superiors will take notice."

Creedmoor shifted his gaze to the ceiling.

"And my superiors, you ask? What a bunch of egotistical, self-indulging, narcissistic morons."

"Hell."

"All my superiors did was micromanage my every move, take all the credit for my ideas, and then stab me in the back."

Creedmoor pointed his finger at Kloet and jabbed the air.

"I tell you, a professional man can only take so much."

"You know, when they pass you over for promotion, they just don't pass you over, it affects your whole family. They pass your whole family over for the basic necessities of life."

Creedmoor shifted his gaze into Kloet's eyes.

"How much motivation do you think someone has, when he works tirelessly and gets passed over time after time?"

"How much motivation do you think someone has when the boot lickers and brown noses get all the credit?"

"I remember back at staff meetings, some senior staff officers could not figure out how to bottle their briefs, so they decided to recite verbatim each and every phone call they received that week," said Creedmoor.

"Can you believe it? The morons! Sitting at an embassy staff meeting going over, word for word, the conversations you had with someone's secretary."

"And, of course, the Ambassador just went along with it. I guess they thought it showed attention to detail."

"Oh, and did I mention how the Chiefs of Station loved being fed tons of metrics?"

"I didn't even know what the word *metric* meant until I already had ten years in, and was back from my third tour in the Far East. But that's what runs the show these days, the metrics. The more metrics you can show, the better."

"All that showed me was that my days were numbered. It showed me that innovative thinkers and guys who loved the field were a thing of the ancient past."

"They squeezed me dry until there was nothing left."

"They love guys who volunteer for everything. Then they use you up and spit you out. They don't give a damn if you show up for work tomorrow, because if you don't, they'll just give your job to some neophyte who they can pay less."

Kloet decided to chip away at Creedmoor's armor.

"Well, I'm all choked up about you Creedmoor. Do you need a hug?" said Kloet.

Creedmoor smiled.

Kloet said, "My life hasn't been the best it could be either. Things didn't turn out exactly the way I envisioned them, but I don't cry about it. I move forward. I try something else. And I would never, ever, sell out my country to Islamic extremists."

Creedmoor listened and thought a moment.

"It all came down to money for me," responded Creedmoor.

"I decided the only way to get even was to make more money than any of those idiots."

"Since my relationships deteriorated to nothing, I realized only money could soothe the pain of my loss."

"Well," Creedmoor continued, "I have the money now. Three million dollars American to be exact. It's all in a safety deposit box in

Brunei. This Philippine mission is a little vacation for me. This is a slight diversion. As soon as this is all over, I'll be back in Brunei."

Creedmoor sat down in the chair across from Kloet again.

"Of course, I don't mind telling you, as you see, you won't be around much longer to tell anyone else."

Kloet looked at Creedmoor and said, "The US won't negotiate for my release. You won't get one dime, Creedmoor, not one red cent."

Creedmoor smiled and said, "You're correct again, Randal. But this is not about money from the US This is about money from Abu Sayyaf. You see, you and Ross have upset quite a few people with your actions in Malaysia. Ross has made many new enemies. This has gone beyond retaliation and anger. This is a matter of pride."

Creedmoor reached into his trousers pocket and pulled out a packet of Marlboro cigarettes and silver Zippo lighter. On the front of the Zippo was embossed the Great Seal of the United States, and the words "US Embassy Kuala Lumpur."

He lit a cigarette and inhaled deeply, letting the smoke linger in his lungs.

Then he tilted his head towards the thatched ceiling and exhaled the smoke.

Staring at Kloet again, Creedmoor said, "Look at this as an old fashioned western bounty on Ross's head. You're just a means to an end, Randal."

"What end?" asked Kloet.

Creedmoor just smiled.

"What end?" asked Kloet again.

"Why, the only, inevitable end that can be. It's the final act in the drama that has been waiting to be played out since last summer."

“What are you talking about Creedmoor?” demanded Kloet.

Creedmoor snarled, “Why, you know. I’m talking about the death of Captain James Ross, of course.”

CHAPTER THIRTEEN

JOURNEY TO JOLO

It was just before nine-thirty in the evening when the taxi carrying Ross and Christianson arrived at Manila Bay pier number six, dock space number one.

Ross got out of the taxi, followed by Christianson.

Reaching into his wallet, Ross pulled out a US twenty dollar bill and handed it through the open window to the driver.

"Thank you sir," said the taxicab driver.

The driver then expertly turned the taxi around and sped off into the night.

There was a lull in the monsoon downpour, and the rains took a brief respite.

Ross and Christianson walked down the aged, creaking gang planks of the long number six pier, noticing the sights and sounds of the Manila Yacht Club adjacent to it.

The Manila Yacht Club was alive tonight.

Yards of brightly colored Chinese lanterns were strung across its entrance. They flickered and illuminated the Yacht Club, giving it a warm, glowing, surreal appearance.

Aromatic smells of delicious international cuisines wafted through its open bay windows.

Bossa nova music was everywhere.

Couples were dining, dancing, talking, laughing, and romancing.

Continuing down the pier, Ross saw the seaplane.

One could not help but notice the ancient looking aircraft docked at the pier's end, around the corner from the flamboyant, upscale Manila Yacht Club.

Emanuel's airplane was a restored US Navy Grumman HU-16D Albatross, formally owned by Pan American World Airways in the 1960s. It had originally been used to fly the Micronesia Islands routes.

Somehow, the plane ended up at Clark US Air Force base, and Emanuel got his hands on it when Clark closed down in 1992.

The plane sported twin radial Wright R-1820-76 Cyclone nine cylinder single row air-cooled engines. It could hold a crew of four to six, and accommodate ten passengers. The Albatross had a maximum speed of two hundred and five knots, and a range of two thousand four hundred seventy-eight nautical miles.

The Albatross was basically an amphibious flying boat. Its fuselage buoyed the craft up by acting similar to a ship's hull. On the Albatross, the hull supported its weight. It maintained stability in the water from the pontoons, or floats mounted to the underside of its wings.

As they got closer, Ross noticed two figures outside the plane. One was Emanuel loading supplies, and the other was a woman.

The woman was Lin Sparrow.

Forgetting why he was there for the moment, Ross ran down the gangplanks and swept Lin up off the ground and into his arms, spinning her around.

Lin eagerly returned the embrace, and then their lips found each other in a long awaited kiss.

Suddenly the world stopped, and nothing else mattered for Ross.

His senses were on overload with Lin's voice, touch, and scent.

Christianson looked at Ross and Lin, and smiled. He walked over to Emanuel and said, "Looks to me like she is more than just a friend."

Christianson extended his right hand to Emanuel.

"My name is Peter, Peter Christianson by the way. You must be Emanuel then?"

Emanuel was looking at the couple and smiling.

"Yes sir, I'm Emanuel. I'm pleased to meet you."

Both men shook hands and continued staring and smiling at the couple.

Ross placed Lin back on the ground and regained his composure.

He made introductions all around.

"Excuse me. Lin, this is Peter Christianson. Peter, this is Lin Sparrow. And I see you both already met Emanuel."

Ross said, "Emanuel, sorry we came a little earlier than I told you we would. I hope you're ready?"

Emanuel was reaching down picking up an ancient looking military footlocker.

He quickly slid it into the open hatchway on the Albatross.

Then he turned around and faced Ross.

Emanuel wiped his soiled hands down the sides of his tattered blue jeans.

"No problem, sir. I'm just finishing loading the last of the supplies I think you will need."

Emanuel looked at his three passengers and beamed a friendly smile.

Staring at their suits, Emanuel quipped, "You gentlemen sure dress fancy for a hunting vacation."

Looking at Christianson, Emanuel said, "By the way, that's quite an interesting family name you have sir. Christianson."

"Does that mean son of a Christian?"

"And with a first name of Peter as well. Oh my goodness."

"Were you named after Peter the Apostle, by chance?"

"I mean, names are indications of who we used to be, and that which we will become, don't you agree?"

"Well, I guess that thought did occur to my parents somewhat," gushed Christianson smiling.

"Isn't that interesting? Peter and James," said Emanuel, "and Lin, being flown to Jolo Island, by Emanuel, for vacation. Now that's quite remarkable, isn't it?"

Ross just listened.

"Well, I'm ready to shove off, if you ladies and gentlemen are ready."

"Wait a minute," said Ross.

Taking both of Lin's hands in his, Ross began explaining.

"Guys, we're not here for vacation, or hunting. I don't want to deceive anyone, and I don't want anyone doing anything they don't want to. Right now, you just have to trust me."

Ross continued.

"It's a long story, but Randal Kloet, a friend of mine, has been kidnapped."

"He's been taken by terrorists, and is being held on Jolo Island."

"He'll be dead in less than forty-eight hours, unless I do something now."

Ross looked at the faces in front of him and corrected himself.

"He'll be dead, unless *we* do something now."

Searching Lin and Emanuel's faces, Ross continued.

"Peter here has agreed to help me. We've got to do something to save Kloet."

Ross looked deeply into the faces.

"We've got to do something. There simply is no more time left."

Emanuel looked at Ross and began to speak.

"Well, my rate just doubled. But I understand. A friend is a friend. A true friend is rare in this world. What you're doing is good. No one should be kidnapped and murdered. No one deserves that fate."

Emanuel beamed a huge smile and reached out his right hand to Ross.

"Maybe when this is all over, I'll write a book and become a Filipino national hero."

Ross grasped Emanuel's hand and shook it firmly.

"I want an autographed copy then," said Ross.

"Right," said Christianson looking at both men. "I think we should get moving."

"Wait a second," said Emanuel.

"Shall we pray?"

Everyone stared at Emanuel.

"A little prayer may come in handy right about now."

Ross looked at Christianson and Lin, and then nodded his head affirmatively.

They all bowed their heads and waited for Emanuel to begin.

Emanuel raised his arms to the dark, foreboding sky, and lowered his head.

"Holy Father, watch over and guide these brave and noble souls on this most caliginous of nights. Safeguard them from the embrace of the Evil One. Grant them the strength of your arm tonight, and let the enemies of darkness not triumph over them. Remember, that only three stand against many, and that only three are not afraid to set the terrible wrong right again. Grant them your victory Father, and protect them with your almighty grace. Righteous Father, I ask this in your most heavenly name, Amen."

Emanuel lowered his arms and raised his head.

"Ladies first," said Emanuel, motioning with his hand for Lin to enter the hatchway on the Albatross.

It was a large step over the metal rim of the entranceway hatch, so she hitched up her dress at its corners to her thighs.

Then she put her right leg through, ducked her head down and under the archway, and glided her left leg over.

Christianson ducked his head and followed Lin through.

Emanuel sort of leaped through the hatchway, as he always did.

Ross was nearly through the hatchway when Emanuel shouted back to him.

“Cast us off, will you sir?”

Ross pulled himself back through the hatchway and walked down the gangplanks to the stern of where the Albatross was moored.

There he undid a mooring rope from an anchor point, then repeated the process at the bow of the aircraft.

Ross couldn’t help but notice the nose art painting on the outside of the fuselage.

Someone had painted a beautiful female angel.

The angel was wearing a sparkling white gown, a halo above her head, and had large outspread wings. At the bottom of her feet was stenciled the words “Saving Grace.”

Ross rolled both mooring lines up and tossed them through the hatchway.

Then he hauled himself back through and closed the hatch behind him.

Once inside, he turned the steel locking hatch lever all the way down and to the right, until it stopped.

The interior of the Albatross was Spartan, but comfortable. Decades ago, Pan American World Airways had outfitted it with ten large plush red leather upholstered seats in two rows running down the middle of the fuselage.

Large brass luggage racks ran across the left and right bulkheads, which were full of Emanuel’s supplies.

Two small white refrigerators were placed side by side in the stern, which Ross was sure were jam packed full of goodies.

Next to the refrigerators was a small teakwood counter, which acted as a bar from which could be served food and drinks.

Strings of twinkling Christmas lights lined the sides and top of the fuselage, which gave the interior a Las Vegas limousine-type ambiance.

Emanuel clawed his way through the cluttered cockpit and plopped himself down into the captain's seat. He automatically released four safety levers, flicked up six toggle switches, and pressed two buttons; breathing life into the twin Wright R-1820-76 Cyclone nine cylinders air-cooled radial engines. Slowly, one thousand four hundred and twenty-five horse power began infusing into each of them.

Emanuel reached overhead and pressed the green intercom switch to the "ON" position.

Static crackled through the ancient overhead speakers aligning the passenger bulkhead of the aircraft.

Ross and Lin sat side-by-side next to each other, with Christianson taking a seat behind Ross.

They were all ears.

"Good evening ladies and gentlemen. Welcome to Air Emanuel. Our flight plan will take us southwest from Manila, proceeding five hundred and thirteen nautical miles southward over the South China Sea, to our final destination of Jolo Island. Refreshments can be had in the refrigerators aft. There you will find an assortment of beers, wines, liqueurs, soft drinks, and juices, along with chips and dips."

The three passengers smiled at each other.

The tourist briefing continued.

"Sorry, but our hostesses are off this evening. You'll have to help yourself once we are airborne. I'll be turning off the interior lights when we are fifteen minutes out from Jolo. I'll let you know when we are exactly six minutes from putting down. So please fasten your seatbelts, and sit back and relax. For those of you who have never experienced a water landing by a seaplane, you are in for a treat. Have a pleasant flight."

The intercom clicked off.

They all buckled their seatbelts in unison.

Emanuel shut off the planes' interior courtesy lights to prepare for taxi and takeoff.

Ross was sitting next to Lin and holding her hand.

He was alone in his thoughts.

What the hell am I doing?

What am I thinking?

I'm conducting an unauthorized rescue mission.

I'm basically violating sovereign Philippine territory.

If I succeed, I'll probably be reprimanded at the least.

And if I fail, I'll have created an international incident.

Not to mention that I could be killed.

But not just me!

I'm bringing along a woman and an old man.

His brow furrowed.

I am responsible for them.

His mind was racing.

But there is no one else.

No one else is going to do anything.

It's only us.

It's entirely up to us.

We have to free Kloet.

There simply is no one else, and there is precious little time left.

Ross knew he was breaking every rule in the officer's guide. He had told Colonel Gautier that he was only going to gather intelligence for SFOD-Delta to mount a rescue mission. He had promised *the old man* that's all he would do.

And here he was, disobeying every rule.

But what is that oldest of rules?

What was it?

Oh yeah.

It goes something like 'combat priorities override everything else.'

Yep, that's it.

Combat priorities override everything else!

The choice was clear to Ross.

He had to do something to save his friend.

He could care less if he received a reprimand, was fired from his job, or drummed out of the service.

His friendship with Kloet was all that mattered now.

But he couldn't help thinking of Lin.

He had never met anyone quite like her before.

He had developed strong feelings for her.

The kind of feelings that might want to make a man settle down.

But could he ever settle down?

Could he ever be happy?

Would he allow himself that luxury?

He had never been in love with a woman before.

Would he allow himself to be in love with her?

Would he be capable, of everything that kind of commitment entailed?

Would he be able to give himself to her truthfully, fully, and completely?

As Ross was thinking, Emanuel was attempting to contact Harbor Control with his two-way transceiver radio. He pressed the "ON/OFF" switch on the handheld black plastic microphone and spoke.

"Hotel Charlie One, this is Echo Alpha Six, come in, over."

He released the "ON/OFF" switch and waited.

There was no response.

He pressed the "ON/OFF" switch again.

"Hotel Charlie One, this is Echo Alpha Six, come in, over."

The man acting in the position as Harbor Master at Harbor Control picked up his microphone and responded.

"Echo Alpha Six, this is Hotel Charlie One, over."

Emanuel said, "Good evening Hotel Charlie One, this is Echo Alpha Six requesting permission to taxi and take off from pier six dock one, over."

"What is your destination Echo Alpha Six, over?"

Emanuel smiled and replied, "Jolo Island for tourism, over."

"Permission granted Echo Alpha Six, over," replied the Harbor Master.

Emanuel said, "Thank you Hotel Charlie One, this is Echo Alpha Six, out."

Emanuel steered the Grumman Albatross seaplane through the water slowly at first, wobbling precariously from side to side as the ocean buoyed it up.

The engine sound started softly and slowly, and then increased in intensity to a high pitched whining crescendo.

Emanuel had tried sound proofing the old planes' interior with foam insulation and paneling. That was so whoever rented his services could carry on conversations without having to shout at each other. But it really was not effective, and as the engine noise increased, so did the passengers' voice octaves.

The Albatross was moving steadily now, and suddenly it lurched forward, with thirty-thousand pounds of aircraft slicing through the sea.

The aircraft was increasing speed steadily, faster and faster, until without warning, it lifted off from the ocean surface like a child's toy being plucked out of a bathtub, and started climbing at a rate of fourteen hundred and fifty feet per minute.

The normal cruising altitude of commercial jet airliners is between thirty-two thousand and thirty-seven thousand feet. The US Navy Grumman HU-16D Albatross had a service ceiling of twenty-one thousand five hundred feet. Since this was a relatively short flight, Emanuel decided to stay at around twelve thousand feet.

The overhead intercom crackled once more with Emanuel's voice as the lights came back on.

"Ladies and gentlemen, it is now safe to unfasten your seatbelts and roam about the cabin. Please feel free to take a look inside the boxes back there. Some things may be of interest to you. And don't forget the snacks! Thank you."

Ross signaled for Lin and Christianson to unbuckle their seatbelts. He stood up and stretched, and then accepted Emanuel's invitation to explore the boxes lining the fuselage.

Actually, the boxes amounted to a combination of old military footlockers and ancient steamer trunks.

The military footlockers were the Vietnam era wooden ones, which had been painted olive drab decades ago, and had names of long forgotten servicemen and their units stenciled across them.

The steamer trunks were even older, mostly wood and vinyl, only much larger.

Ross walked around the passenger seats and squatted down next to the first trunk in his path.

He unbuckled two sets of leather straps and let them hang loose.

Then he pried open the ancient container with his fingers.

Inside was a curious item that Ross was not expecting to find.

The box contained a Self Contained Underwater Breathing Apparatus, or SCUBA compressed air tank.

From the looks of it, it was very old, probably from the 1970s.

It was a seventy-two cubic foot version, made out of steel, with an old US Divers Company J-valve threaded onto it. The J-valve was the old school reserve air valve allowing a diver to release an extra amount of air when he started to run low. Modern SCUBA aqualung tanks were not equipped with J-valves, because today's divers all used submersible pressure gauges or dive computers to monitor their air consumption.

The tank had the standard US Navy black shoulder strap harness.

Next to the SCUBA tank was a mesh weight belt which had been corroded from sea salt. Sixteen pounds of lead weights had been secured to the belt.

Two underwater knives lay in the trunk as well. They each were stainless steel, with serrated-edge and black hard rubber handle. The knives were in black plastic sheaths with straps to secure to your leg.

Also in the trunk were a divers black rubber facemask, a pair of black rubber adjustable-heal US Divers rocket fins, and a US Divers two stage Aqua-Master double hose regulator.

Next to the regulator lay a US Navy Mark 31 Model O Signal Projector, and seven screw-in flares. The Mark 31 was basically the size of your average ballpoint pen, hence the term "pen flare."

This is all old standard US Navy issue gear, probably acquired from Subic Naval Station when it closed down, thought Ross.

He moved on to the next trunk.

The contents were pretty much the same.

Inside, he found a vintage set of twin SCUBA steel seventy-two aqualung tanks, which utilized the US Divers twin manifold with J-valve. The tanks had the standard Navy black mesh shoulder strap harness. Also in the trunk were a similar double hose regulator, mask, fins, and a weight belt.

Along with some underwater wrist compasses and diving knives, this trunk also contained about a dozen US Navy Mark 13 Model O Signal Flares. These were five and one half inch long cylindrical distress flares, which housed orange smoke on one side and bright red illumination on the other, accessed by pulling a pin on either side.

Inside the next trunk was something very unusual.

It contained an old US Navy Emerson-Lambertsen Closed-Circuit Oxygen Underwater Breathing Apparatus.

This Emerson Underwater Breathing Apparatus, or UBA, is a closed-circuit oxygen breathing lung, officially designated as a recirculating UBA. It is a rebreathing unit which is virtually bubble free, commonly used by combat swimmers for missions requiring undetected approaches. Compressed air units are known as open-circuit when they disperse bubbles to the surface, while closed-circuit recirculating units do not release bubbles.

The Emerson rebreather rig consists of a carbon dioxide absorption canister with an oxygen supply cylinder mounted on the swimmers back, and a gas-flow regulating assembly with breathing bags and breathing hoses attached to a nylon vest mounted on his chest.

The Emerson rig had been replaced by the Navy for quite some time now, and this one had to be at least thirty-five years old.

Next to the Emerson rig were also a diving mask, fins, weights, and weight belt.

Several pieces of paper were also folded up inside the trunk.

They were old, weathered, crumbling, and yellowed sheets of instructions from the Naval Training Center at Dam Neck in Virginia Beach.

The instruction sheets had a date stamped on them. It read "31 July 1971."

Underwater diving with compressed air SCUBA was different than diving with a rebreathing unit. For instance, the deepest that a normal, healthy person should dive on compressed air was around one hundred and thirty feet. This is based on several factors, but mostly because of the amount of nitrogen that is absorbed at depth by the body. Back in the day, not much diving was done below forty feet with a closed-circuit UBA. This is because the breathing medium is oxygen as opposed to compressed air, and the potential for oxygen poisoning is increased at depth.

Christianson was walking around and exploring as well.

He bent down and pried up the rusty hasp on one of the footlockers and opened the top.

Inside were several pistols with ammunition.

There were two M1911A1 Colt forty-five ACP caliber pistols. They were the parkerized military version with "United States Property" stamped on the receiver.

Next to these, were three Smith & Wesson Model 13 revolvers in thirty-eight special caliber. These revolvers sported two inch barrels, and had the words "Property of US Air Force" stamped into the metal on the back tang of the handle.

Alongside of the pistols was a pile of about two hundred rounds each of the caliber forty-five and thirty-eight special, which appeared to have flayed out when their ancient cardboard boxes had deteriorated over time.

Christianson closed the lid and open the next footlocker.

Inside were four M3A1 submachine guns in forty-five ACP caliber. These were commonly referred to as the "grease gun" because of their similar appearance to an auto mechanics greasing tool.

Next to the M3A1's were around twenty long-stick magazines capable of holding thirty bullets each.

Lin had been following Ross around and peering into the boxes.

She gently placed her hand on Ross's left forearm.

There were several questions that Lin wanted to ask Ross, such as how were they going to find Kloet in this typhoon, and how were they going to free him once they did find him. But as she watched Ross examine the supplies, she felt a chill run down her spine and decided against asking.

Lin thought about Ross and what was happening.

Here is a guy who is going to rescue his friend against all odds.

He doesn't even know what odds are aligned against him.

He is going to risk his life for a friend.

Why?

Only a very special person does that, someone who believes in themselves and in the justness of their cause.

Lin knew *Ross was that kind of man.*

She recognized that *he was more intense than other men she had met in her life.*

Ross was unusually serious.

Ross would rather have nothing, than lie about something.

He was truthful and didn't lie about who he was or what he wanted.

Ross didn't waste his time *acting the jerk* like other men she had dated.

Ross seemed to use his life to do what was right.

He did not waste his talents on mediocrity.

Ross had deep reserves of psychological strength and character.

He seemed to take the harder road, and actually relished it.

The key to Ross's discipline was his honor.

Mostly though, Lin felt that *Ross was a totally sincere man.*

And the biggest thing that appealed about Ross to Lin was that *she felt safe with him.*

When things got rough, Lin would stick with Ross and all would be well.

She would pick Ross over anything.

Lin secretly dreamed she would love to have a dozen children with the man.

Clearing her mind, Lin asked, "What can we expect when we reach Jolo?"

Ross reached up and ran his fingers through his hair to brush it back off of his forehead. But it just fell back down again, only in more disarray this time.

Ross looked at Lin and Christianson. He motioned for them all to take a seat. He sat down in front of them and explained the operation.

"It should be cut and dried to find the house where Kloet is being held."

Ross reached into his trousers pocket and pulled out the piece of paper with the address.

"The house is at five-seventeen Bata-Bata Road. It won't be hard to find. Jolo is a very small island. The residents are very clannish, and almost every household has firearms. That will be to our advantage."

"Several years ago, we conducted Operation ULTIMATUM and cleared the island of about four hundred terrorist guerrillas. Since then, we've been conducting foreign internal defense missions and generally have been winning over the populace."

"So, here's what we're going to do …"

CHAPTER FOURTEEN

TENDER KISS

The weather was getting worse and worse as the flight drew on and on.

The typhoon winds were sucking in the monsoon rains and making quite a mess of Emanuel's flight plan.

The Grumman Albatross was being buffeted back and forth by the violent gusts, and drenched by the sloshing rains.

Emanuel was holding the old girl steady though, like a father patiently teaching his child the fine art of riding a bicycle.

The inside of the plane was like riding on a rollercoaster.

The passengers were continually rocked to and fro in their seats, and at one point Lin turned her head to the side and retched.

The sounds of the twin Wright Cyclone engines seemed to be amplified and penetrating the skin of the aircraft. They were becoming more and more a screaming contest with the roar of the typhoon winds.

Ross looked at his battered Benrus.

Its luminous military dial told him it was twenty-two-thirty hours in the evening now.

He glanced through a portside window and could see nothing but pitch blackness and rivulets of rain.

The interior courtesy lights went out as the intercom crackled with static.

"Ladies and gentlemen, we are making our final approach to Jolo Island," said Emanuel.

"Please fasten your seatbelts as it may get a little bit bumpy, so hold on back there."

Ross reached over and held Lin's hand. He kissed it tenderly.

"Lin, you're going to remain on the plane with Emanuel until this is over. It's just too dangerous for you to come with Peter and myself."

"But…."

"I'm sorry Lin, but that's the way it has to be. It's just too dangerous."

Christianson looked at them both and nodded his head affirmatively.

The Albatross suddenly lurched to the left, as if Zeus himself agreed and was playing with them like a yo-yo on a string.

Emanuel brought the plane back on line and proceeded to rapidly descend.

Ross looked out his portside window.

It was a gloomy view, racked by lightning and buckets of rain, but he could make out scattered lights twinkling from the numerous islands below.

How Emanuel could distinguish which island was Jolo was beyond anyone's comprehension.

The Albatross was descending faster and faster as the storm outside was slamming against it and whipping the aircraft hither and thither from side to side.

Unexpectedly, Emanuel pulled the plane's nose up, and time itself seemed to be suspended for five or six-seconds.

Then the plane and everyone's stomachs dropped, and they could feel the Albatross's belly slap on the ocean's surface like a blue whale after it has breached.

Now the Albatross was slicing through the South China Sea and making way for a discreet cove that Emanuel had used numerous times in the past.

"Ladies and gentlemen," crackled the intercom, "we are now approaching the Jolo coast. Please remain seated until I get this heavenly angel bedded down. Thank you."

The twin Wright Cyclone engines continued their high pitched whine for another two minutes and then abruptly shut down.

As the Albatross bobbed in the ocean, Emanuel came back through the main cabin and opened the port hatch.

He made sure the mooring cable line was secured to the cathead, and then threw the anchor out and overboard. The anchor sank down until its fluke snagged the bottom.

"Well, here we are," said Emanuel.

"Mister Ross, sir, I've got a Mark 4 Navy life raft in the stern. Let me get her for you."

"Wait up there Emanuel, let me help you. You can't do all the work yourself," said Ross.

Emanuel smiled and said, "Okay, follow me."

Emanuel led the way to the tail of the Albatross. Ross noticed him stop in front of a musty old gray tarpaulin. Emanuel reached over and pulled the tarp off, revealing the deflated Mark 4 life raft.

"Here we go, let's pick her up," grunted Emanuel as he and Ross squatted down simultaneously and reached for the life raft.

They picked it up and walked forward to the port hatch.

"Lay her down, sir," said Emanuel.

Ross complied, and then Emanuel slid the raft through the hatch and out into the water.

Holding on to the raft by its guide rope, Emanuel hung outside the hatch and pulled a pin on a compressed air canister which immediately inflated the Mark 4.

Leaning back inside, Emanuel secured the guide rope to a deck anchor point.

The rain was still coming down in sheets outside.

"Time to get whatever equipment you and Mister Christianson need, sir," said Emanuel with rain mist stinging his face through the open hatchway.

Ross looked at Christianson, who was already bending over footlockers and separating the weapons and equipment into two piles.

Christianson's face became deadly serious before he spoke.

"I figure a grease gun with three sticks of ammo for each of us. That gives us each two reloads. That should be enough for the heavy artillery. We can conceal them under our suit coats. We have our choice between the Colts' or the Smith & Wesson handguns. You'll probably want the Colt, but I'll stick with the Smith & Wesson. I hope it doesn't get to where we actually have to use the pistols, but if we do, I figure we should each carry enough ammo for two reloads. Personally, I think you just can't beat an old wheel gun. And we'll each take two of the flares to signal Emanuel and Lin when we've got Kloet and are coming back. One will be used for backup, just in case."

Christianson looked at Ross and raised an eyebrow.

"Well, what do you think, Jim?"

Ross could remember, not too long ago, when he would blindly trust the leaders of his country. He had closed his mind to anything and anyone, other than government officials and the military, as ever measuring up to his standards.

And now, here he was, acting on his own.

His country and all its mighty Armed Forces had decided to do nothing to save his friend Randal Kloet.

The only people who he could count on in this moment of crisis, in this time of decision, were an old man, a taxi driver, and a nurse.

His whole outlook was changing about people, courage, and honor.

Ross understood more than most that you don't have to wear a patch on your shoulder to be a hero, and that you don't need to be saluted to have honor.

He was starting to feel emotional now, and he forced his mind to control it.

Ross smiled and said, "Peter, I think that's the best damn brief-back I ever heard. Let's do this."

Ross took off his suit jacket.

He filled three M3A1 submachine gun stick magazines each with thirty .45 ACP caliber cartridges.

Next, he put seven more bullets each into the M1911A1 Colt magazines, and inserted one magazine into the pistol. He pulled the slide back and let it snap forward, allowing a bullet to be chambered. Then he flicked up the Colts' safety lever with his right thumb.

Picking up the grease gun, he slung it by its strap around his shoulder so that it was just under his right armpit.

Then he put his jacket back on, and slipped the Colt into his waistband behind his belt buckle.

Emanuel saw what was happening and scurried back into the cockpit. He emerged with two bags and said, "Here you go. Use these empty Claymore mine bags to carry your handguns, extra bullets, and flares."

Both Ross and Christianson stared at Emanuel and were not surprised that he had military issued bags that used to hold Claymore mines.

"What?" Emanuel asked.

"I use these to hold my toothpaste and shave stuff."

Emanuel handed them each a dark green bag with a shoulder strap. The bags were about the size of a medium ladies purse.

Ross put his pistol, ammunition magazines, and flares into the bag and snapped it closed. Then he slung it around his shoulder.

Christianson secured his equipment the same way, and then gave Ross the thumbs up signal.

Ross bent down and took off his socks and shoes. He tied the laces together in a square knot and then hung the shoes around his neck.

“Peter, take your shoes off and tie them together and hang them around your neck. That way you won’t lose them in the surf.”

Ross stuck out his arm to shake Emanuel’s hand, but Emanuel wrapped his arms around him in an embrace instead. Ross felt a strange sense of comfort and renewal in Emanuel’s embrace, as if he had been infused with additional courage.

And then it was over.

“Be seeing you in a bit,” said Ross.

“Yes sir, I’ll be here.”

Ross turned his attention to Lin.

Her white summer dress was soaking wet from the rain and now clinging to her body. She had kicked off her sandals moments before and stood there, barefoot and shivering, with a look of extreme desperation on her face.

A look of desperation, like someone who was about to lose everything they had ever cared for, and didn’t know what on earth to do about it.

Lin was terrified about what was going to happen, but she knew she had no control over it.

Lin knew Ross.

She knew no one could stop Ross, even if it meant him losing his life.

Ross would do what he had to do to make things right.

That’s why Lin admired Ross.

No matter what forces fate had transpired against him, Ross would keep going and never quit.

To Lin, Ross was beyond the pettiness of most people.

Ross was the most genuine human being she had ever met.

And now, here he was, putting himself in harm's way again, and Lin was powerless to do anything to help him.

She became overwhelmed by the emotion of the moment, and her eyes suddenly filled with tears.

Lin spontaneously reached up and wrapped her arms around Ross's neck and pulled him close.

"I love you James," she said.

Lin closed her eyes and her lips met his in a tender kiss.

It was a kiss that no force on earth could tear asunder.

It was a kiss that heaven's angels could envy.

It was a kiss that could turn darkness into light.

It was a kiss that God himself could smile at.

Ross allowed his nostrils to fill with Lin's luxurious scent. It intoxicated him, and for a second he was swirling through time and space.

There was no present, no past; no danger, no enemy; no regret, no despair.

There was only the kiss.

But then the moment was over, and he reached up and took Lin's arms from around his neck.

"You need to stay here Lin, and be ready. Randy will need medical attention when we bring him back. He'll need your life-saving skills. You're the only one that can do it."

Lin nodded her head up and down in agreement.

"Emanuel will watch out for you Lin," said Ross.

"Right now we've got to get moving. And I promise you that we'll be back soon."

Ross turned around and climbed through the hatchway and crawled out into the life raft. He reached up and helped Christianson get settled.

Emanuel threw the guide rope over and Ross caught it. As Ross was securing the guide rope, Christianson found the oars and handed one to Ross.

Strangely, the drenching monsoon rains had stopped to all but a drizzle now, and there was a curious lull in the vicious typhoon winds.

Both men stuck their oars into the dark ocean waters and started paddling towards the beach and the lights on shore.

CHAPTER FIFTEEN

FOR A REASON

Lin and Emanuel had a chance to talk while Ross and Christianson were on their mission.

"They'll be back soon, Lin. Please, sit with me. Would you like something to eat or drink?" asked Emanuel, playing host.

"Sure. Do you have orange juice?" asked Lin.

"I do. Come on. Have a seat."

Lin sat down in one of the large plush red leather upholstered chairs in the middle of the fuselage. Emanuel went to the stern and opened one of the small refrigerators and took out a cold carton of orange juice. He bent down, reaching behind the teakwood bar, and then straightened up with two paper cups in his hands. He filled both cups with orange juice, and then walked over and sat down next to Lin.

Handing Lin a cup, Emanuel asked, "So Lin, how long have you known Mister Ross?"

"Not long," answered Lin. "Not long at all really."

"Well, he seems like a fine gentleman," said Emanuel. "He seems like the kind of man you can trust to take care of you."

"Yes," said Lin.

The strings of twinkling Christmas lights lining the sides and top of the fuselage gave the interior of the Albatross a bizarre yet friendly ambiance. Emanuel left the lights on, shining through the windows, as a navigational aid for Ross and Christianson.

Emanuel studied Lin for a few seconds. His eyes seemed to look all around and over her, from top to bottom. Finally he spoke.

"You have an aura about you, Lin. There is a feeling I get, that you are a gifted woman. Your mind is open to everything, isn't it?"

Lin gulped down the remains of her orange juice.

"I don't know. I guess so," said Lin.

"It's good to have a fresh, compassionate, open mind. It's good to not be prejudiced by doctrine and dogma. You can only learn if your mind's eye is open," said Emanuel.

"They say that people who have such auras can see things that others cannot. They say, that people who can see things that others cannot, are blessed. But some people see that blessing as a curse."

"And that's you, isn't it, Lin?"

Lin said, "I suppose that's true. People have been afraid of me at times."

Lin normally did not just open up and discuss her life with anyone, but this was different.

Somehow, she got the feeling that she could trust Emanuel.

Lin said, "When I was a child, I'd been accused of practicing witchcraft, because I had visions. Because I saw things that others didn't. But my father believed in me. He used to say I had the gift. But people become afraid of what they don't understand, don't they?"

Emanuel smiled.

"There are many things that cannot be explained in this world and the next, Lin. Even after several lifetimes, we never really stop learning. There are many things that people do not understand. People are sometimes brought into your life for a reason. Usually that reason is to teach you something. Sometimes, you learn the most when you least expect it."

"I agree Emanuel, I agree," said Lin. "But sometimes I wonder why God allows all this evil to go on in the world."

Emanuel just listened.

She looked at Emanuel curiously.

"And so, why are you helping James with all this? Why are you risking your life?" asked Lin.

Emanuel smiled.

"Because he needed a tour guide," he said.

CHAPTER SIXTEEN

DEAD MEN PAY NO FARES

The surface of the ocean had calmed down considerably at this late hour as the Mark 4 life raft cut its tiny swath through it.

The strenuous paddling, stroke after stroke, went on for several minutes, and then finally the surface ocean waves broke and they were in the surf zone.

"Jump out now and we'll pull her in," yelled Ross to Christianson.

Ross leaped over the side of the life raft and his feet hit sand, but Christianson had a little trouble. He wobbled at first, and then slipped and flopped over the side. He came up coughing and spitting out saltwater.

Remembering who he was and trying to regain his composure, Christianson said, "That was refreshing."

"Grab a side handle and we'll pull her in," said Ross.

With knees pumping and churning through the silt, both men shuffled forward and hauled the raft up and onto the beach.

They strained and pulled at the life raft, as if their tendons would rip from their arms.

Finally, after covering about fifteen meters, they were able to beach the raft securely.

"Are you all right, Peter?" asked Ross.

"Yeah, no problem," replied Christianson out of breath.

The men crouched down near the life raft and put their shoes on over their sand-encrusted feet.

Ross checked his watch.

It was eleven-fifteen pm.

The macabre darkness of the night was pierced by the moon's sprinkling of its eerie green luminescent glow on the beach, giving the sands an unearthly effervescent shimmer. A slight misting of rain continued to tease at Ross and Christianson.

Ross got his bearings and scanned the shore.

Off in the distance, Ross could see the twinkling lights of the town of Jolo. About twenty-five meters to their right was a dirt road, with what appeared to be a taxi stand of some sort at its junction.

Ross motioned to Christianson and both men stood up.

They walked side by side towards the taxi stand.

Ross ran his fingers through his hair in an attempt to brush it off of his forehead. But it just fell right back down again, only in more disorder.

The wind had ceased now, and the rainy mist still stung at their faces.

Both men looked a site worse for wear.

Maybe the taxi driver will think we just got caught in the storm, thought Ross.

As they sauntered forward, the taxi stand came into clearer view.

The stand wasn't much to look at. It consisted of a ten foot by ten foot slab of concrete, with eight foot tall metal poles at each corner rising up to a corrugated tin roof, on which someone had painted the red and white diving flag symbol.

It appeared that the taxi stand had been built and rebuilt many times, and Ross was surprised it was still standing during the typhoon.

Inside the stand, scattered around helter-skelter, were four small rattan chairs and a foldout card table. A Coleman lantern hanging from a hook in the roof was the sole source of light, and one got the idea that nowhere could there be found a motivated taxi driver to brave the elements of this typhoon for a fare.

Nothing could have been further from the truth.

Parked right behind the structure was a taxi.

It was the typical Jeepney taxi found everywhere throughout the Philippines.

Inside the Jeepney sat the driver, who upon seeing Ross and Christianson, immediately got out and said, "Are you gentlemen looking for a ride somewhere?"

The driver was a Filipino man who was at least seventy years old if he was a day. The man was about five feet two inches tall. His hair was white and thinning, and his face had a dark leathery appearance as if he had spent the majority of his life being beaten by the elements. He was wearing a white open collar Guayabera shirt. The shirt had two vertical rows of alforzas fancy stitched pleats running down the front. The old gentleman had his sleeves rolled up to his knobby elbows. Dark blue trousers hung loosely on his lithe hips. The whole ensemble was topped off with weather beaten brown sandals on his calloused feet.

"My name's Trece. Where do you gentlemen wish to go? Maybe you're looking for a nice hotel, or a good restaurant?"

"Where do you wish to go?"

"It's a terrible night to be out, don't you think?" said Trece.

Ross reached into his trousers pocket and pulled out a small piece of paper. He handed it to Mister Trece.

"Take us here," said Ross.

Trece studied the piece of crumpled paper.

"Oh yes, okay, five-seventeen Bata-Bata Road. I know where this is. It's right around the corner. Sure."

"Come on," said Trece.

Trece shuffled around and held the right front passenger door open. Ross reached in and tilted the seat forward to allow Christianson to climb in the back.

Trece waited for Ross to get seated and then closed the passenger door. He scurried around and seated himself behind the rather large steering wheel.

"Okay gentlemen, here we go," said Trece.

Trece inserted his key into the Jeepney's ignition switch, turning it to the right.

The engine rumbled slightly at first, coughing and sputtering, and slowly came to life.

Then Trece put the Jeepney in gear and, turning on the headlights, steered expertly around the taxi stand and onto an unimproved dirt road, heading east.

Ross scanned the sides of the road for street names but couldn't see any.

"What road is this?" asked Ross.

"We're on Sawaki Boulevard now sir," answered Trece.

Some boulevard, thought Christianson in the backseat of the Jeepney.

"Up ahead is Bayog Road, and then we will be on Bata-Bata," said Trece.

"We'll be there in about ten minutes."

Ross looked at his watch.

The luminous hands of his Benrus said eleven-thirty-nine pm.

Ross turned around and looked at Christianson.

"Peter, when we get to the house, we need to split up. I'll take the front, and you go around and cover the back."

Christianson nodded affirmatively.

Ross continued.

"I'll go in first. I wish there wouldn't be any shooting, but there probably will be. The terrorists holding Kloet are killers."

"Make no mistake about it, they won't hesitate to kill."

"And, neither will we."

"When you hear the shooting, get in there quickly anyway you can."

"But if something happens to me, just get Kloet and get back to the plane."

Christianson said quietly, "Nothing's going to happen to you Jim. We'll make it."

Trece pretended not to pay attention to their conversation.

These Amerikanos are looking for trouble, thought Trece.

He kept his eyes glued to the road.

He had heard it all before.

He had seen many things happen while living in the Philippines.

He had lived through insurrections.

He had lived through revolutions.

He had lived through wars.

He had come to realize that none of it made any sense.

To Trece, all the fighting for causes was just a waste.

It was all bad for business.

After all, *dead men could not pay their fares.*

The clan-based society of Jolo made it extremely difficult for the police to enforce any kind of law and order.

And Trece had driven countless men into gunfights.

He had driven countless men to their deaths.

What Trece always made sure of, first and foremost, was that he always collected his fare.

Trece finally spoke up.

"Ah, sir, it's going to be four hundred and twenty-five Pesos, sir," said Trece.

Ross reached behind him into his trousers left rear pocket.

He pulled out and opened a small plastic waterproof zip-lock bag that held his wallet.

"Let's see," said Ross. "That's about ten bucks."

Ross extracted a hundred dollar US bill and handed it to Trece.

"Here's a hundred dollars American. There's another hundred for you, if you can wait around and drive us back."

Trece took the hundred dollar bill and smelled it.

"Why yes sir, I'll wait for you and drive you back."

"It will be my pleasure sir," said Trece, smiling as he folded the bill and tucked it into his Guayabera shirt pocket.

Ross turned his attention back to the road.

He scanned the streets and noticed the effects of the typhoon. It seemed that everywhere there were palm branches strewn across the roads. The palms were covering the muddy furrows that had been cut by the rivulets of water from the monsoon rains.

The triumphant return to Jerusalem, over the palm branches, thought Ross.

He quickly dismissed the thought from his mind.

Ross said, "How much longer until we get there?"

Trece looked back and forth across the street and began to slow down. He pointed with his finger to the left as the Jeepney came to a halt in front of several houses that were indistinguishable from each other in the night.

"It's the middle house, over there sir," said Trece.

Ross looked at the house.

There was no one to be seen around it.

There were no sounds at all.

It was quiet.

It was too quiet.

The house looked deserted except for the tiny beam of light emanating from under the front door.

It really is just a shack, thought Ross.

He was surprised it had not been blown down by the typhoon.

"Okay Mister Trece. Wait right here for us please. And thanks," said Ross.

"I'll be right here sir, don't worry."

Ross turned around and looked at Christianson. He pulled out his submachine gun and motioned for Christianson to do the same.

Both men loaded their weapons.

Ross got out of the Jeepney and held the door open for Christianson.

They were about fifteen meters away from the front of the house.

Ross could not see any signs of guards or sentries anywhere.

"Time to split up," whispered Ross.

Christianson broke off to the right, keeping a distance of about five meters from the house, and crept around to the rear.

Ross slowly walked to the front of the house.

The door looked like it was made of split bamboo. It had a brass doorknob on the right hand side, underneath which was a key lock.

There was no time for reconnaissance or second thoughts.

There was precious little time left before Kloet was to be killed.

Ross had no idea of knowing how many rooms were in the house, or exactly how many terrorists there were.

His experience in the art of close quarter's battle told him that he just needed to bust in the door and sweep the room, left to right, clearing the entire house, room by room, until he found Kloet.

And Ross trusted the experience and professionalism of Christianson, being a retired Secret Service Agent.

Ross always positively identified his targets before he fired, and he understood Christianson would do the same.

He took a deep breath in through his nostrils, and let it out slowly through his pursed lips.

Ross looked down at his M3A1 submachine gun once more, and verified that the bolt was to the rear and the weapon was ready to fire.

NOW!

Ross charged forward, leading with his left shoulder, and smashed through the door.

The door splintered apart with an earsplitting cracking sound and swung wide to the left, slamming against the wall.

Ross sprang like a tiger inside and automatically crouched down to lower his target silhouette.

He immediately identified three men sitting in chairs around a small table in the middle of the tiny room, and leveled his submachine gun at them.

But the men stayed seated and did not move.

Two of the men were Caucasian, and the other man was Filipino.

They were all neatly groomed, and well dressed in suits and ties.

One of the Caucasian men was around forty or forty-five years old, with gray hair. The other two men were in their early thirties.

The Filipino man on Ross's right side stood up and spoke first.

"Captain Ross, I'm Special Agent Nestor Lukban of the National Bureau of Investigation."

The Special Agent flipped the wallet in his hand open and displayed his badge and credentials.

"And you're under arrest for violating the Sovereign Neutrality Act of the Philippines."

CHAPTER SEVENTEEN

THIRTY PIECES OF SILVER

Ross kept his submachine gun leveled on the three men.

His mind was racing.

What the hell is this?

"Where is Randal Kloet?" demanded Ross.

Both of the Caucasian men stood up simultaneously.

The older looking one introduced himself.

"Ross, my name is Clive Maxsted. I'm Special Assistant to the US Ambassador here."

Maxsted motioned with his thumb to the other Caucasian man.

"This here is Special Agent Erwin Foxwell, of Diplomatic Security," said Maxsted. "As Agent Lukban said, you're under arrest for violating the Sovereign Neutrality Act of the Philippines."

Ross was stunned.

Special Agent Foxwell began saying, "You have the right to remain silent …"

Ross couldn't believe what he was hearing.

Ross exclaimed, "You've got to be kidding!"

Foxwell said, "Put your weapon on the deck, slowly, Captain Ross. Then place your hands on your head and take one step back."

Maxsted snapped back, "Do as you're told soldier, because right now you're in for a world of hurt the likes of which you have never seen!"

Ross resignedly lowered his submachine gun to his side, but continued to hold it by the pistol grip with his right hand.

"You can't be serious," said Ross. "I'm here to secure Randal Kloet. I had verified intelligence that he was being held prisoner here, by Abu Sayyaf."

Maxsted yelled, "That's the point Ross! You are not a rescue squad! You have no charter for this type of operation!"

Slowly, deliberately, Special Agent Foxwell said, "Put the weapon down now."

Foxwell flicked back his coat tail with his right hand and drew out his Sig Sauer P-228 nine millimeter pistol.

He aimed the pistol at Ross.

These guys are pulling the rope tight. It's going to snap unless I give them some slack.

Ross allowed his submachine gun to drop, making a *"thud"* sound on the dirt floor of the shack.

"Place your hands on your head."

Thinking quickly, Ross replied, "I'm here on official orders from First Special Forces Group."

Foxwell jabbed the air and pointed at Ross with his left hand index finger.

"Place your hands on your head," repeated Foxwell.

Ross's mind was swirling.

"Call my Commander, Colonel Gautier. He'll verify why I am here and what my mission is."

Maxsted laughed out loud.

"Colonel Gautier! That fool! He's gone Ross."

Ross stared at Maxsted incredulously.

"What do you mean?" demanded Ross.

Maxsted said, "Colonel Gautier has been moved out of command because of this little stunt of yours."

Ross could feel the rage boiling inside himself.

To control his emotions, he took a deep breath and slowly let it out.

"That can't be possible," said Ross.

"Oh it sure is possible," replied Maxsted.

"Gautier should have been court-martialed for this, but he's going to be allowed to retire," said Maxsted.

Ross thought to himself deductively.

Buy some time here.

Don't upset these guys further.

Think!

Convince them to let you go.

Ross reluctantly placed his hands on top of his head and took a step back.

Foxwell continued pointing his handgun at Ross.

Special Agent Nestor Lukban was silently taking in the entire scene.

This doesn't make any sense, he thought to himself.

These embassy guys used me to arrest this Captain.

I didn't want to arrest him.

I told them they should just warn the guy.

He is just trying to save his friend.

Maybe he acted outside his jurisdiction a little, but we should not arrest him.

A warning would have been good enough.

We should let him go.

Hell, we should help him!

Lukban was not used to seeing the good guys get beat up.

Maxsted said, "You know Ross, you're lucky on the one hand. We're taking you back to the US Embassy, instead of letting Special Agent Lukban lock you up in a Philippine jail."

Lukban was beside himself.

They're really going overboard now, Lukban thought to himself.

"Ross, you'll be on the first embassy flight to the US in the morning," said Maxsted.

Ross thought quickly.

Try their emotions, he speculated.

"What about Randal Kloet? He's an embassy employee. He'll be dead unless we do something now!"

Maxsted just stared at Ross and smirked.

"What's wrong with you, Ross? Kloet is not your concern! You know, this country has laws too! You just can't violate them whenever you feel like it!"

Maxsted was enjoying himself now.

"Who do you think you are, Ross? You think that Green Beret on your head is a license to do whatever you want? Do you think that Special Forces soldiers are untouchable?"

Ross couldn't believe what he was hearing.

"Well I'm personally going to see to it that Fort Bragg takes away that little qualification from you. I'm going to see to it that you're drummed out of the service, Ross."

Jesus this is crazy now, thought Lukban.

This guy may have stretched the rules a little, but he doesn't deserve this.

Maxsted turned his attention to Foxwell.

"Special Agent Foxwell, please handcuff Mister Ross and escort him outside to our car. I'm tired of this nonsense."

Foxwell nodded his head affirmatively and started to move forward towards Ross.

Ross looked at the ground and was desperately thinking what else he could do in this hopeless situation.

Just then, the room became eerily silent.

Something grabbed Ross's attention and he looked up.

What's that?

On the opposite side of the room, Ross saw a small flash of light flickering from underneath the rear door.

The light grew larger and larger, and then suddenly the rear door burst open.

"Hold it."

The words were crisp and clear, and the tone of the voice emanating them was cold and deadly.

Ross smiled broadly.

It was Christianson.

CHAPTER EIGHTEEN

RUSE

"Everybody just take it easy," said Christianson.

The old Secret Serviceman was standing in the middle of the rear doorway in his black suit, white shirt with thin black necktie, and black wingtip shoes.

His thinning white hair was tousled about on top of his head.

His eyes were bloodshot, yet still brilliantly blue-gray.

And he was dripping wet all over.

Christianson aimed his Smith & Wesson Model 13 revolver at the nearest threat, which happened to be the armed Agent Foxwell.

Maxsted, Lukban, and Foxwell all turned around to face him.

There was a look of astonishment on their faces.

Special Agent Foxwell immediately recognized that Christianson was exhibiting the classic Weaver Stance of combat pistol shooting.

And he was aiming his revolver at Foxwell.

Seeing this, Foxwell lowered his pistol to his side.

"Everybody relax and take it easy," said Christianson.

He then reached inside the left breast pocket of his suit jacket and pulled out his wallet.

He flipped it open to reveal his Secret Service badge and credentials.

Maxsted, Lukban, and Foxwell all stared at the five pointed gold star in disbelief.

Ross lowered his hands to his sides.

Christianson said, "I'm Special Agent Peter Christianson of the United States Secret Service, and you gentlemen have made a gross mistake here."

"You see, Captain Ross could not tell you what his priority mission is, because of National Security concerns."

Christianson looked at the men.

The expression on his face remained deadpan.

"It was on a need to know basis, and I'm sure you can appreciate that."

Maxsted was ready to explode.

"What the hell is all this?" Maxsted blurted out.

Christianson said, "All I can tell you is that Captain Ross here is assisting us on an official Secret Service matter."

Maxsted was furious.

"What the hell are you talking about? Ross is under arrest!"

Christianson remained calm and professional.

"No sir, I'm afraid he's not."

"You see sir, Captain Ross here is assisting us in an investigation of an assassination plot against the President of the United States."

"Now I respect your rank in the State Department sir, but since this is a federal matter involving a threat against the President, well, that's really all I can let you know, sir."

Maxsted's jaw dropped open.

Foxwell holstered his Sig Sauer pistol and sighed deeply.

Lukban was so relieved he just simply smiled.

Ross looked at Christianson in wonder.

Christianson said, "Captain Ross, we're on bit of a tight schedule, and we need to get moving. We have a plane waiting."

"Gentlemen," said Christianson, with a nod of his head.

He then walked across the dirt floor and motioned for Ross to follow him.

Ross reached down and picked up his M3A1 submachine gun.

He gave the briefest of glances at the three stunned men in front of him, and then abruptly turned around and quickly followed Christianson out the front door.

Maxsted's face had become flushed with embarrassment. It slowly started to return to its natural hue. He looked at Foxwell and Lukban, while regaining his composure.

"Well I'll be God damned."

"Gentlemen, we did our job here, as best we knew it. But, it has always been my experience that situations change constantly," said Maxsted.

Maxsted focused his gaze on Lukban.

"Thank you for coming down here to assist us in this matter, Nestor. Your services will no longer be required. Thank you again," said Maxsted.

He shook Special Agent Lukban's hand vigorously.

Then Maxsted narrowed his focus to Foxwell.

"Let's get back to the hotel, Erwin. I'm beat," said Maxsted.

CHAPTER NINETEEN

WET WORK

The atmosphere outside the shack was unearthly.

There was an eerie, grotesque murkiness to the night.

The sky was pitch black, yet curiously comforting.

The air was moist and sticky, and clung to Ross and Christianson like a witches spell.

As they made their way through it, Christianson said, "Come on James. Let's get the hell out of here."

Ross and Christianson both began trotting hastily towards the taxi.

Trece saw the two men rushing rather rapidly towards his location. He immediately got out of his seat and scurried outside to open the passenger door of the Jeepney for them.

"How did it go gentlemen?" asked Trece.

Ross pulled out a hundred dollar bill from his wallet and slapped it into Trece's hand.

"Take us to the beach where you picked us up, as fast as you can please," said Ross.

Trece shoved the hundred dollar bill into the breast pocket of his Guayabera shirt.

"Yes sir."

Ross held the passenger door open as Christianson climbed into the back and collapsed into the vinyl seats.

As soon as Ross was inside, Trece turned the key in the ignition and gunned the engine.

He turned his head right and then left, scanning the streets for any cars, and then spun the steering wheel and made a racing u-turn.

Trece drove the Jeepney like a professional chauffeur through the midnight blackness of the Jolo streets.

Ross thought about what had just transpired.

The old man did it. He came through in the clinch.

He turned to look at Christianson.

Christianson was crumpled in the back seat, breathing hard.

"Thanks for that back there, Peter. You saved my skin."

Christianson straightened himself up in the back seat and caught his breath.

He took a deep breath, held it for a second, and let it out slowly between his lips.

"You're welcome James," said Christianson.

"Peter, did you plan it, I mean, when to enter the room, or was it coincidence?" asked Ross.

Christianson leaned forward.

"I was inside the back room just before you broke in. The door was unlocked."

"Unlocked?" asked Ross.

"Yeah, unlocked," answered Christianson.

"Anyway, I heard the conversation taking place. I knew I had to get in there, but I also knew I had to finesse these State Department guys."

"So, I came up with the Presidential assassination ruse."

Ross was listening intently.

"It's just a matter of conditioning and discipline," said Christianson, "and luck."

Ross smiled for a second, and then his expression became serious.

"Well, we still struck out trying to find Kloet. Right now, I have no idea where to look for him."

Trece was concentrating on his driving, but he was also listening to their conversation.

These Amerikanos did not find their friend.

That means he will be killed for sure.

And after he is killed, it will mean more trouble for my beloved Philippines.

There is no reason for this man to be murdered.

These terrorists are just gangsters.

No one is safe as long as these gangsters run wild.

These gangsters need to be stopped.

This insanity needs to end tonight.

Trece spoke to Ross while keeping his eyes on the road.

"Ah, excuse me sir, but perhaps I may be of assistance to you," said Trece.

Ross turned and stared at Trece.

"How's that sir?" Ross asked puzzled.

"I think I can help you out. May I make a phone call?" asked Trece.

Ross understood that Jolo was a tight knit community where everyone knew everyone else's business. It was very clannish with deep running family relationships.

"Okay," said Ross.

Ross turned around and looked at Christianson with raised eyebrows.

Trece's cell phone was lying on the dashboard buried amongst crumpled candy wrappers and receipts. He plunged his hand into the pile and scooped it up.

Glancing at his contact numbers, Trece scrolled through them and stopped at one annotated with a star symbol. He pressed the button and waited.

Trece spoke on the phone utilizing the Tausug dialect, which is indigenous to the Sulu Archipelago.

He asked several questions, and listened for a few minutes.

Then he shut the phone off.

Ross and Christianson were waiting in silence with bated breath.

"Well sir, I have some information for you. I was just talking to my cousin, who is a good man, and he is very good friends with a close associate of the Sulu Governor. My cousin is also close friends with a trader out of Marunggas. Well, some people say he is a smuggler, but I don't believe it. I've seen his import and export license. He is an international trader. Anyway, he knows some, ah, young men, who like to get into trouble. And, he says your friend was taken to the abandoned lighthouse."

Ross was trying to follow the convoluted conversation, and finally just shook his head.

"What abandoned lighthouse?" asked Ross.

"It's the lighthouse near Olongapo on Subic Bay, sir. It's very old, built in 1905 I believe by the Spanish government. It's on Sueste Point, sir. The lighthouse and the keeper's house are not used anymore. They're in a shambles. The lantern tower still works, but hasn't been operating for years. It used to be a spot where young people hung out at night, and did what young people do. Your friend was taken to this lighthouse. It's on the west side of Subic Bay, near the entrance, on a promontory point. You can't miss it. The only way to reach it is by boat, sir."

"Are you sure he's being held in this old lighthouse?" asked Ross.

Trece smiled.

"Yes sir, I'm sure. My cousin said this man, Kloet, was moved there over three hours ago. He also said there were four men guarding Kloet, and that the leader is a white man."

"But there's one thing that is really interesting about this lighthouse," said Trece.

"What's that?" asked Ross.

"Well sir, this abandoned lighthouse has an underwater entrance," explained Trece.

"Underwater entrance?" asked Ross.

"Yes sir. You see, the west side of Subic Bay is quite rocky. That's why the lighthouse was built on the headland. There is some beach access, but mostly the shore terrain is high and jagged. So, back in 1905, the Spanish built a flight of concrete steps rising from the sea to the lighthouse. Underneath the steps they built a tunnel which was used as an access point to the shore in case of terrible weather like a typhoon. The only problem was it began to flood all the time. Over the years the tunnel started to be abused by vandals. Now it looks pretty much like a sewer from the lighthouse, which empties out into the bay. Well, the entrance to the tunnel is right under the steps."

Ross thought for a moment.

"Is the entrance large enough for a man to walk in?"

"Yes sir. It is a little narrow, and some places you may have to hunch down, but you can walk the whole way underground to the lighthouse. The only problem is the flooding sometimes," said Trece.

"Is it hard to find the concrete steps at night?" asked Ross.

"Not really sir. There is a huge flag pole with the Philippine flag flying atop it right next to the bottom of the steps. It must be at least a hundred feet tall."

Now the taxi stand came into view, and Trece expertly steered the Jeepney around it, and parked in the front.

Ross got out and held the front seat forward to allow Christianson to exit.

The weather was turning again, and the moist air became a chilling mist.

Ross walked around the taxi and stood in front of Trece.

Ross wondered whether he should believe Trece and the information he provided about Kloet.

After all, it could be a trap.

But he decided he really had no choice. Kloet had less than forty-eight hours to live.

There simply was nothing else to do, except trust Trece and get to Olongapo as quickly as possible.

Ross extended his hand, and Trece's face lit up with a warm, friendly smile.

"I have told you the truth sir, believe me. I have no reason to lie to you. I hate these gangsters who have ruined my Philippines. They have turned Jolo into a war zone. My grandchildren can no longer play in the streets safely. The sooner their influence leaves my island, the better it will be," said Trece.

"Thank you, Mister Trece," said Ross. "We're going to try our best to get rid of these gangsters for you and your people."

The two men shook hands.

Then Trece reached out and embraced Ross.

Seeing this, Christianson walked over and shook hands with Trece as well.

Trece said, "Be the repairers of the breach, gentlemen. Good luck to you both."

Christianson turned his collar up to the cold and looked at Ross.

"Time to go Jim?" he asked.

"Yeah, let's move," said Ross, with a final wave of his hand to Trece.

They turned from the taxi stand and walked towards the coast.

The chilling mist turned to rain again, and it pelted their faces as they churned their silt-filled shoes through the sand in search of the raft.

Soon they were at the life raft and struggling to pull it back down the beach.

The moon shined its luminescent beams across the ocean with a shimmering malevolence. The surface was calm, even still, as the rain stung into it deeply with its needles.

Christianson, in particular, was enjoying every minute. He hadn't felt quite this alive in a long time.

He did not want the moment to end.

He felt aches all over his body that he hadn't felt in a long, long time.

He just hoped he could keep going.

His years in the Secret Service had conditioned him, through discipline, to make his body do what it normally would not.

They reached the shore, and hoisted the raft up and over the foamy surf and into the sea.

The Albatross could be seen off in the distance due to its twinkling lights.

Both men sunk their oars into the water and started paddling towards the lights.

Ross and Christianson were soaking wet again.

If I never get wet again, it will be too soon, thought Christianson to himself.

CHAPTER TWENTY

OLONGAPO LIGHTHOUSE

The trip to Olongapo was quiet.

Ross was lost in his thoughts.

Olongapo, meaning "head of the elder" in the Philippine language of Tagalog, got its name from an ancient legend of warring tribes and the decapitation of a wise old man who tried to bring the tribes together. According to the popular legend, beheading was an acceptable form of getting rid of a person whose views were opposed by the Sambal people.

Ross knew the legend.

He understood why this was the method of assassination that the Abu Sayyaf and Jemaah Islamiah terrorist group members chose for Randal Kloet.

It will make a political statement that the United States and its policies are evil and must be destroyed.

Ross had gone over his rescue plan for Kloet with everyone before they took off. The idea was for Emanuel to land in Subic Bay as stealthily as he could, and as close as he could to the abandoned lighthouse. Ross and Christianson would use the life raft to get close to the shore, while constantly checking for sentries. If there were no visible sentries or guards, then the concrete steps would be used all the way to the lighthouse. If there were too many sentries, then they would swim the rest of the way underwater through the tunnel system, utilizing SCUBA. Once in the lighthouse, they would clear the building from bottom to top, until they found Kloet.

Ross knew it was risky, but every military mission is.

He looked at his Benrus watch.

Its luminous military dial read two-thirty in the morning.

Ross rose up out of his seat and walked to the cockpit.

"Would you care for some company?" Ross asked.

"Sure sir, please have a seat," said Emanuel.

Ross sat down in the co-pilots seat to the right of Emanuel.

The instrument panel was lit up, and it seemed that Emanuel was surrounded in the cockpit by every conceivable type of gauge, dial, light, switch, button, and lever.

He looked like a mad scientist.

"Tell me Emanuel, what do you know of the Sueste Point lighthouse?"

"Well sir, it was a 'candle against the darkness' as they say, wasn't it? It hasn't been operational for years. But on special occasions like holidays, they sometimes crank her up and let her shine all night. I've heard about the submersible entrance before too. You have to watch for the tides around there, but you should make it. Your plan sounded pretty good."

"Thanks. How long until we get there?" asked Ross.

"Oh, another fifteen minutes or so, Boss," said Emanuel.

"Okay. Thanks," said Ross.

"Wait," said Emanuel.

Emanuel plunged his left hand into the pilots' kit bag at his side and rummaged around for a second.

He pulled out a plastic Chem Light and handed it to Ross.

"Here, this may come in handy," said Emanuel smiling.

"Thanks," replied Ross pocketing the light.

Ross got up and left the cockpit.

He walked down the passageway of the fuselage to where the main seats were.

Ross sat down next to Lin.

"Hey Lin, how are you holding up?"

Lin reached out and grasped Ross's hand, clutching it.

"I'm worried, James. How do you know what to expect at the lighthouse?"

Ross thought about her question for a few seconds.

"Well, I have the information from both Mister Trece and Emanuel to go on. Don't worry Lin. Everything will be all right. We'll get Randy out of there."

Ross raised Lin's hand up to his lips and gave it a gentle kiss.

"Everything will be fine, I promise," said Ross reassuringly.

"I know, I know. But I'm just so worried about you and your friend Peter. I'm worried about everyone. I've tried to project my thoughts to the end of this thing, but I just can't. I can't see an outcome."

Ross smiled confidently.

"That's because the future is not set, Lin. We can change it, just as we're going to change it tonight. We're going to make the future our own."

In the cockpit, Emanuel reached overhead and pressed the green intercom switch to the "ON" position.

Static crackled again through the ancient overhead speakers aligning the passenger bulkhead of the aircraft.

"Ladies and gentlemen, we are six minutes out of Subic Bay, and in the process of making our final descent. Please prepare yourselves. Thank you," said Emanuel's voice through the speakers.

The interiors lights went out as Ross, Christianson, and Lin buckled their seatbelts and prepared for the water landing.

Outside the weather was getting worse.

The typhoon winds had started gusting halfway through the flight to Subic.

Emanuel's flight plan was getting soaking wet again as the monsoon rains returned.

The Albatross was being buffeted back and forth as it descended lower and lower.

Emanuel continued holding the old girl steady, like a father patiently teaching his child the fine art of swimming.

Sitting inside the aircraft and taking all the jolts reminded Ross of twisting through a water slide at Sea World.

The screaming contests between the sounds of the twin Wright Cyclone engines and the roar of the typhoon winds returned and penetrated the skin of the plane.

Ross looked at his battered Benrus.

It was almost three o'clock in the morning.

He peered through a portside window and could see nothing but pitch blackness.

The Albatross began violently lurching right and left, but Emanuel brought the plane back on line and proceeded to rapidly descend.

The descent became faster and faster as the storm outside increased in intensity.

The tiny aircraft was whipped and wracked violently back and forth for the second time this evening.

Everyone inside the Albatross could feel Emanuel suddenly pull the plane's nose up, as time seemed to suspend itself for four or five seconds.

Then the plane and everyone's stomachs dropped, and the Albatross's belly slapped on the ocean's surface like a submarine after an emergency ascent.

Now the Albatross was slicing through the South China Sea and making way for Sueste Point.

"Ladies and gentlemen," crackled the intercom, "we are approaching Sueste Point. I attempted to request permission to land, but could not get through even on the emergency frequencies. It must be due to interference from the typhoon."

The silhouette from the Sueste Point lighthouse could be seen looming over the rocky coast.

Emanuel continued taxiing towards it.

He steered the Grumman Albatross seaplane through the water, slowly at first, wobbling precariously from side to side, as the ocean buoyed it up.

The twin Wright Cyclone engines continued their high pitched whine for another thirty seconds, and then Emanuel abruptly shut them down.

They were about seventy meters from the coastline.

As the Albatross bobbed in the open sea, Emanuel raced back through the main cabin and opened the port hatch.

Making sure the mooring cable line was secured to the cathead, Emanuel threw the anchor out and overboard.

The anchor plummeted down, until its fluke snagged the bottom of the sea.

Emanuel didn't say a word as he looked at Ross, Lin, and Christianson. He just made the sign of the cross with his right hand, bestowing his blessing on them all.

Ross walked to the stern and knelt down beside one of the steamer trunks.

He unbuckled two sets of leather straps and let them fall to the sides.

Inside the trunk was the US Navy Emerson rebreathing unit.

Ross hauled out the rig and laid it down on the deck.

He began checking to make sure everything was in working order.

"So you're going to use that rebreather to swim through the sewer to the lighthouse?" Christianson asked Ross.

"Tunnel," corrected Ross smiling.

"But you're right. I'll use the closed-circuit rig, and you'll use the open-circuit, or normal SCUBA gear. I'm going to set you up with the single tank. The double tanks may be too big to be able to pass through the tunnel system," said Ross.

"Okay," said Christianson. "I'm a PADI certified diver as well, so I know how to use SCUBA gear. It's been awhile believe me, but I know how."

"Good," said Ross.

Next, Ross set up and tested the SCUBA equipment for Christianson.

Both systems were functioning properly.

"We'll only use pistols on this trip, Peter. The submachine guns will be too heavy to lug around if we have to go underwater. Put your revolver and extra ammo in your Claymore mine bag again. That'll secure it in case the tunnel is flooded and we have to go submerged," said Ross.

Christianson removed the M3A1 submachine gun from around his shoulder. Then he pulled out the Smith & Wesson Model 13 revolver and swung open the cylinder. He checked to see that it was fully loaded, and then slapped the cylinder shut.

"Right," said Christianson.

"Shoes tied together and hung around the neck again?" asked Christianson.

"Yes," replied Ross. "We don't want to risk losing them in the water if we get swamped and have to swim for it."

Both men took off their socks and shoes. Then they tied the laces together and hung their shoes around their necks.

Ross noticed Christianson's feet. They were all cut up and bruised from the pounding they took in the life raft and on the beach. Every step he took left a bloody footprint.

Christianson didn't say a word.

During their hasty departure from Jolo Island, Emanuel had quickly deflated the Mark 4 life raft, and pulled it through the hatch with Ross's help. Once inside the plane, he installed a new compressed air canister to the raft.

Now, Emanuel and Ross pushed the deflated raft once more through the hatch, and watched as it slapped harmlessly onto the ocean's surface.

Emanuel hung outside the hatch and pulled the pin on the life raft's compressed air canister.

Immediately the Mark 4 inflated.

Then he secured the guide rope of the raft to a deck anchor point inside the Albatross.

Ross leaned out the hatch and placed the diving gear into the raft.

Lin was standing and nervously rubbing her hands together.

Along with the gift of clairvoyance, Lin had a sort of sixth sense about death.

She could feel it.

At times, she could see it in her dreams and visions.

But now, she sensed it everywhere.

She felt it in the plane.

She felt it all around her.

Lin couldn't shake the feeling.

Death was coming tonight.

Death was waiting.

Death's arms were open, and wantonly anticipating an embrace.

Lin couldn't shake the feeling, and it frightened her.

Christianson saw Lin was troubled, and he stepped over to her and fatherly embraced her.

"Don't worry Lin. I won't let anything happen to Jim. And we'll get Kloet out as well. Believe me," said Christianson.

She looked at the old Secret Serviceman in the black suit and white shirt.

She looked at his black wingtip shoes.

She looked at his thin black necktie with the golden PT 109 tie clip.

She looked at his thinning tousled gray hair on top of his head.

She looked into his bloodshot, yet still vibrant blue-gray eyes.

Lin smiled a worried smile at Christianson.

"Everything will be fine. You'll see. I've been doing this all my life," said Christianson.

He leaned in close and pressed his lips to her ear.

"I promise you, he'll be all right," whispered Christianson.

"I promise you. I'll protect him."

Lin returned the embrace, as if that gesture would somehow guarantee the outcome she desired.

Christianson released his arms from around Lin. He walked over to Ross and looked him in the eyes.

"It's time to do this," said Christianson.

Emanuel looked at Ross and said, "Do you guys need anything else? Is there anything at all I can do for you?"

"No. That's it," said Ross. "All the gear checks out fine. Just watch out for Lin."

Ross walked over to Lin.

Her white summer dress had been destroyed by the monsoon rains, and clung to her like wrinkled Saran Wrap.

Ross grasped both of her hands in his.

"We'd better get moving, Lin. But we'll be back with Randy as soon as we can," said Ross.

Emanuel moved over beside Christianson, and both men looked at the young lovers.

Ross reached around and gently pulled Lin close.

Lin responded by wrapping her arms around Ross.

Ross closed his eyes and leaned in, tenderly kissing her.

Lin returned the kiss.

Ross was immediately enveloped by the warmth of her sweet embrace.

He yearned to surrender to its overwhelming passion.

For an instant, nothing else mattered.

For a moment, everything was clear.

Nothing else existed in the world.

Time stood still, and everything was as it should be.

And then it was over.

Ross gently pulled away, and motioned to Christianson.

With Ross leading the way, Christianson followed him out through the Albatross's hatch and into the bobbing life raft.

Emanuel untied the guide rope and handed it to Ross through the hatch.

Both men got situated, and then sliced their oars once more into the choppy waters of the South China Sea.

At three o'clock in the morning, it was malignantly gloomy outside. The monsoon rain had returned, and brought streaks of lightning with it. The typhoon winds were picking up, and it was beginning to get difficult to hear each other speak.

Ross yelled to Christianson, "This sure is one crazy typhoon. The weather changes every hour!"

"Yeah, it provides us with good cover though. These damn Abu Sayyaf guys won't even see us coming!" yelled back Christianson.

Ross set his azimuth on the silhouette of the old lighthouse, which Trece said was their target.

Its tower structure was foreboding against the night sky. Originally painted white, the lighthouse was now a moss green and rusty mosaic of French and Spanish architecture.

Ross could clearly see the twisted cast iron cupola, and the stone ruins of the outbuildings. He could also see that there were lights on inside.

To Ross, the sinister shape looked like something right out of an Edgar Allan Poe story.

The jagged coastline was coming up quickly, and now Ross could see the tall flag pole with the Philippine colors violently flapping against the wind. The huge concrete steps were right next to the pole, and acted as a respite inland from the treacherous sea.

Ross and Christianson paddled viciously and steered the life raft back and forth through the current.

The cold rain pelted their bodies and stung at their faces.

Lightning was flashing across the horizon and belching thunderous cracks through the sky.

As they got closer, both men observed silhouettes highlighted on the horizon, of what could only be armed patrolling sentry teams.

They were around ten meters from the shore now, and Ross could see a sandy opening at the base of the steps to moor a small craft.

"There it is!" yelled Ross over the howling of the winds.

Christianson nodded, and both men paddled strenuously and steered their raft towards the mooring point.

The life raft unexpectedly surged forward from the current, and Ross dropped his paddle and jumped out with the guide rope in his hands.

His feet dug deeply into the sand, and he pushed forward and saw where a metal anchoring post jutted up through the earth.

Christianson heaved his body over the side, and both men pulled and pushed the raft inland.

Ross wrapped the guide rope around the ancient barnacle-encrusted anchoring stump, and secured it tightly. Then he turned around and helped Christianson pull the raft in until it was fully beached.

Christianson crouched down beside the raft and caught his breath.

Ross took a knee and put his hand on Christianson's shoulder.

"Are you all right, Peter?" asked Ross.

"Never better," gasped Christianson.

"Did you see the guards patrolling?" asked Ross.

"Yeah," said Christianson. "There were about four or five teams of two each. They were all over the horizon. There are a lot more than Trece talked about. Maybe they even have some kind of early warning system installed," said Christianson.

"Could be," said Ross. "Let's find that tunnel entrance then. Come on."

Ross and Christianson stood up and moved as a team to where the concrete steps buttressed the sea.

"Wait here," Ross told Christianson.

Ross pulled his diving mask over his face and took a breath. He submerged underwater for a look.

The good news was the tunnel entrance wasn't hard to find.

The concrete steps ended at the mouth of the sea. Built into the concrete directly below the steps was a huge cast iron grate. The grate originally had iron bars every foot or so built into it. Over the decades, the saltwater had corroded and deteriorated the bars to where they were only stubs now.

The bad news was the entrance was completely submerged.

Ross surfaced and gave the details to Christianson.

"It looks simple enough. We just put on our gear and head up the shaft," said Ross.

"What if it's locked on the other side?" Christianson asked.

"Then I'll just shoot the lock off with my forty-five," answered Ross.

"Piece of cake," replied Christianson.

Both men went back to the raft, took off their laced-together-shoes from around their necks, and pulled out their underwater swimming gear.

Ross turned on each of their air supplies and checked them by taking a breath.

"They're good," he said.

Ross picked up the SCUBA tank and held it while Christianson pulled the harness straps over his shoulders and secured them around his waist and chest. He tied a quick release in the straps in case he would have to emergency jettison the cylinder underwater.

Bending down, Ross picked up the Emerson rebreather and handed it to Christianson.

Christianson held the rebreather steady while Ross slipped his arms through the olive drab colored nylon vest, pulling it down and zipping it up.

One by one, each man reached over and supported the other while they bent down and pulled their fins over their bare feet.

The ordeal of the day was taking its toll. Both men's clothes were torn and soaking wet. Their bodies were cut, bruised, and rubbed raw from the ever present grating sand. They were encrusted with sticky sea salt. And they were becoming exhausted.

Though it was raining, each man was sweating profusely from the exertion and stress.

God let me be able to finish this, thought Christianson to himself for a second.

Then he immediately dismissed the thought from his mind.

Ross's Special Forces training had kicked in, and he was on autopilot.

Now they pulled their diving masks down over their faces and put their regulator mouthpieces in between their lips.

Ross held up his right hand and displayed the international diving "okay" symbol to Christianson, who then did the same.

Leading the way, Ross sunk down to his knees, and then completely submerged beneath the black surface.

Ross waited a second, and Christianson followed.

Then both men swam into the tunnel entrance.

Once they were both inside, Ross pulled the Chem Light out of his Claymore mine bag. He held the cylindrical tube with both hands, and quickly snapped it in the middle breaking the capsule inside. Then he shook the plastic light vigorously back and forth for a few seconds.

The Chem Light ignited and emitted an eerie yellowish-green glow.

The water temperature was tepid, and they had to swim single file through the cramped, unearthly murky shaft, illuminated in front for a few feet only by the welcome glow of the Chem Light.

Ross led the way, with Christianson following so closely that Ross's fins would sometimes slap him in the face.

But there was only one way to go.

Forward.

Forward.

Forward.

Ross was continually scanning all sides of the tunnel for underwater dangers.

They had swum about thirty meters into the macabre darkness when, unexpectedly, the silt at the bottom of the shaft stirred in front of Ross's eyes.

It became alive with movement.

The sediment was sinisterly shifting back and forth, and then erupted in a frothy cloud.

To Ross's surprise, a young stingray rose up out of the blackness.

With a powerful thrust, the stingray flapped its triangular wing-type pectoral fins in front of his face.

As quickly as it had appeared, the grayish-blue stingray disappeared beneath Ross and skirted past Christianson.

It was all so fast, that Christianson could only stare with controlled curiosity at the stingray as it passed.

Ross kept his knees straight and continued flutter kicking his legs from the hips.

Kicking.

Kicking.

Kicking.

Onward.

Upward.

Forward.

Ross turned around every few meters to check on Christianson. The old man was right there, keeping up.

The only sounds to be heard in the underwater tunnel were the rasping and hissing of the two men's diving regulators.

As Ross was swimming, his left wrist was dragging too close to the sides of the tunnel. His wristwatch strap became snagged on a sharp protruding object. Whatever the object was, it sliced the leather band in two. Ross's beloved Benrus watch was snatched from his wrist, and floated down disappearing into the muddy bottom.

After about seventy-five meters of underwater swimming through the murky black ink, Ross could now distinguish the end of the tunnel.

He held the Chem Light above his head and saw shafts of light wafting down from some kind of opening.

Ross turned to Christianson and stuck up his thumb, displaying to him the international "ascend" diving symbol.

Christianson returned the sign and gave Ross the "okay" symbol with his fingers.

Underwater, Ross opened his Claymore mine bag and pulled out his Colt automatic. He clenched his fingers around the hand grip, and straightened his right arm upwards with the pistol. He ascended with his arm extended over his head. This was in case there were sentries present, and so that his fist would encounter any obstructions first on the way up instead of his head.

One by one, each man swam up and broke the surface.

With his pistol and facemask above the water level, Ross quickly scanned the scene.

He did not see any guards.

It appeared as if they had surfaced in some kind of underground chamber.

Using his palms, Ross shoved himself up and out over the ledge and took a knee. He pulled off his diving mask and scanned the room once more, only this time thoroughly reassuring himself no one else was there.

They had surfaced in the old cistern room of the lighthouse.

This stone room had been dug underneath the lighthouse like a basement. Over one hundred years ago, the lighthouse keepers used this as their storage room. From the looks of the walls, it appeared as if the cistern room flooded a lot.

The room was pretty sparse. There were some stacked wooden barrels and a few old rotten wood chairs scattered about in the corners. Ancient stone steps led up to the first deck. High up in each corner of the walls was installed a single light bulb encased by a small protective wire cage.

A good idea, thought Ross. The lights allowed him to see the numerous rats scurrying about.

Ross turned around and placed the Colt on the floor. He bent down to give Christianson a hand.

Grabbing a hold of Christianson's SCUBA tank, Ross pulled him up and out of the tunnel opening, and stood him up.

Christianson pulled his harness strap quick releases and allowed the aqualung to slide from his back. He bent over and laid it down gently so as not to make any noise.

"We're not going to be able to use this gear to get back to the plane with Kloet, so let's just ditch it here," whispered Ross.

"Okay," whispered Christianson, pulling his diving mask off his face.

Ross unzipped the vest of his Emerson rebreather and squirmed his shoulders through it.

Silently, each man tied down his mask and fins to his breathing apparatus using their harness straps. Then they moved over to the edge of the underwater tunnel opening. One by one, they eased their equipment into the black waters of the underground tunnel and watched it disappear.

"It still looks like a sewer to me," whispered Christianson, as he drew out his Smith & Wesson thirty-eight special revolver.

Ross bent over and picked up his Colt from the cold wet floor. He pulled the slide back a quarter of an inch and looked to verify that a round was chambered. Then he allowed the slide to ease forward and cocked the hammer back.

There was only one door in the cistern room. It was a massive oak door whose bottom and sides were rotted from constant exposure to all the moisture and mold. The door was at the top of the primeval stone steps.

Ross pointed up to the door.

"Let's go," he whispered.

Christianson followed as both men climbed up the steps and stopped on the landing in front of the mammoth door.

Ross stood on the right side of the door frame. He held the Colt pistol in his right hand, and gripped the corroded brass door handle with his left.

Christianson positioned himself on the left side of the door frame. He gripped his revolver utilizing the classic combat pistol technique.

Ross nodded his head up and down three times.

He firmly pushed, and the timeworn door inched open effortlessly.

Ross peered inside for a second, and then threw the door open wide.

"Jesus," said Ross.

CHAPTER TWENTY-ONE

RESCUE

Ross and Christianson were taken aback by what they saw.

It was the body of a man with silver duct tape over his eyes.

The body was placed next to the wall inside the room, and was lying on a gurney.

There was no one else in the room.

At the head of the gurney were two wooden chairs and a small foldout table, which had a deck of playing cards scattered about on top of it.

Sitting on the table was an electric brass lamp plugged into a wall socket.

Behind the table stood a five foot tall metal pole from which hung a bag of intravenous fluid.

Plastic tubing ran from the bag to the body, and was surgically taped to his left arm.

Christianson stood guard while Ross walked over to the body and knelt down.

Ross leaned over and removed the duct tape from the man's eyes.

The man was Randal Kloet.

Ross reached over and shook him on the shoulder.

"Randy, Randy, it's me, it's James," said Ross.

Kloet's eyes fluttered open and attempted to focus.

"James? Jamie? Is that you?" whispered Kloet.

"It's me all right Randy. I'm here with Peter Christianson. We're gonna get you out of here."

Ross looked up at the intravenous bag. He saw the words *VECURONIUM BROMIDE* printed on a white label stuck to the center of the bag.

He had no idea what vecuronium bromide was, but it didn't sound good.

With his eyes, Ross traced the intravenous tubing to Kloet's left forearm. He yanked up the surgical adhesive tape and pulled out the plastic catheter from the inside of Kloet's vein. Then he reapplied the surgical tape and applied pressure on Kloet's arm to stop the bleeding.

"Come on Randy, let's get you up. We've got to get moving. Can you stand?" asked Ross.

"Yeah, okay, I don't know. I think that drug paralyzed me, Jamie," said Kloet. "I mean, I could see and hear what was going on, but I just couldn't move."

He struggled, but Kloet could barely sit up.

Ross and Christianson put Kloet's arms around their shoulders and helped him to his feet.

Randal Kloet weighed one hundred and eighty-five pounds of muscle. He was wearing faded blue jeans and a maroon open collar sport shirt. His feet were bare. If his shoes were in the room, Ross couldn't see them.

The room Kloet was being held in was circular with white plastered walls. It looked as if it were part of the cylindrical ascending tower.

"This room has got to be above ground," said Ross.

In the center of the room was a spiral metal stairway leading to a trapdoor in the wooden ceiling above their heads. Ross surmised that this next level above them was the watch room, which housed the clockworks for rotating the lenses of the upper lantern room.

Built into the wall behind the stairway was another wooden door.

"That door has to be the way out of here," said Ross.

No sooner had Ross spoken, than above them through the ceiling could be heard the sounds of someone walking back and forth.

"Quiet," whispered Ross as he placed his finger to his lips.

The *"clip-clop, clip-clop"* sound of the footsteps above them echoed through the wood ceiling and reverberated off the spiral metal stairway. It soon was in competition with a metallic *"klackety-klackety"* sound.

Someone on the higher deck was fiddling with equipment of some sort.

Ross whispered, "We'll use the cover of darkness and the storm to make our way down to the raft, and then to the plane. But we'll avoid the steps, as they'll probably be heavily patrolled."

"That sounds good. That sounds like a good plan. We'll make it," whispered Christianson.

Together, Ross and Christianson walked Kloet to the door. They were trying to get him to move his own legs, but he couldn't. They basically just ended up dragging him.

There was a brass doorknob on this door with a keyhole lock directly beneath it. Ross tried to turn the doorknob, but it would not budge. It was locked.

"I've got this," whispered Christianson.

Ross supported Kloet's weight, and both men watched Christianson.

Christianson removed his PT 109 tie clip from his necktie. He pulled the retaining pin off of the back of the tie clip and straightened it out. Then, with his left hand, he inserted the straight end of the clip into the lock. He pushed it to the left while maintaining constant pressure on it as a tension bar. With his right hand, he inserted the retaining pin into the lock mechanism. Slowly, he twisted and turned the pin up and down for about twenty seconds. Then he pulled the pin up and to the left, while applying pressure. The lock made a *"snap"* sound.

Kloet asked, "Who *are* you, Peter?"

Christianson replied with a deadpan face.

"I'm just an American."

"Ready?" said Christianson. He had his left arm back under Kloet's right armpit and around his back. The Smith & Wesson revolver was in Christianson's right hand.

"Yeah," replied Ross. His right arm was under Kloet's left armpit, and he held the Colt pistol in his left hand.

They had no idea of knowing when the paralytic effects of the vecuronium bromide drug would dissipate from Kloet's system. He still could not walk or support his own weight with his legs.

Kloet turned his head to the right and looked at Christianson, and then turned to the left to look at Ross. Then he squeezed both of their shoulders with his hands.

"Come on guys. Let's get the hell out of here," said Kloet.

Christianson turned the doorknob to the left and pulled the door open.

The three men walked through the doorway and were almost blown back inside by the wind.

The typhoon was wrecking havoc outside.

It was soon clear to Ross why no Abu Sayyaf agents were guarding Kloet. There was no need to since he had been paralyzed from the vecuronium drug, and the storm outside was enough to keep him from going anywhere.

Now it was a race to the shoreline and freedom.

The man-made pathway looming in front of them was constructed mostly from gravel and crushed coral.

Every step reminded them that they were not wearing shoes.

Ross, Kloet, and Christianson were moving like guys in a three-legged race.

They were walking him, pulling him, and literally dragging Kloet to the shore.

The rain was drenching them once again, and the wind whipped at their clothes like a test pilot in a centrifuge.

The darkness of the night was erased at intervals by brilliant flashes of lightning streaking across the sky.

The resonance of the violent winds was in competition with the earsplitting cracks of thunder.

The three Americans kept moving and were making progress slogging through all of it.

Suddenly, a great beam of illuminating light descended upon them, and for a second Ross thought it was a lightning strike.

He turned his head and looked up.

It's the lighthouse beam!

Someone had activated the lamp and lens, and now turned it on the three of them.

High up in the lantern room, Julius Creedmoor was aiming the beam of illuminating light on the escaping threesome.

"Kill them! Kill them!" screamed Creedmoor through a shattered glass storm pane from the lighthouse tower.

"Kill them all!"

There were five roving teams of terrorists patrolling the headland. They heard the commotion and saw the activated lighthouse beam sweep the grounds. Immediately they descended to the scene like a pack of ravenous wolves searching for a kill.

The keeper's living-quarters house was located adjacent to the lighthouse. Yellow lights flashed on inside it, accompanied by the sounds of people shouting in Arabic.

"Allahu Akbar!"

"Allahu Akbar!"

"Allahu Akbar!"

The front door abruptly slammed open, and men started pouring out.

Ross and Christianson were desperately holding Kloet up.

They turned around to see what was happening.

"Damn it," cursed Ross.

At least twenty screaming Abu Sayyaf, Jemaah Islamiyah, and Al-Qaeda operatives brandishing AK-47 assault rifles stormed out of the building.

"Allahu Akbar!"

"Allahu Akbar!"

"Allahu Akbar!"

These twenty men, and the five roving teams, meant there were at least thirty terrorists attacking the trio of Americans.

Ross heaved Kloet up onto his shoulders in a fireman's carry.

"Come on Pete let's go!"

Both men ran, side by side, trying to reach the life raft and escape.

The terrorists were not sure how many infidels had defiled their domain, since the illuminating light beam suddenly disappeared off the surface of the ground.

Creedmoor had zoned the lighthouse beam on the escaping trio but for a mere few seconds. Then his bloodlust got the better of him, and he decided to leave the tower to join in the hunt.

Now the lighthouse beam was back up and rotating around and around in the lantern room as it normally would.

Creedmoor pulled out his Sig Sauer pistol and ran down the metal spiral stairway like a possessed madman.

Ross and Christianson moved as fast as they could with the cover of darkness concealing them once again.

BAM!

BAM!

BAM!

BAM!

BAM!

The terrorists had opened fire with their AK-47 assault rifles in the vicinity of where the intruders had been observed.

Angry wasps of hot lead were zipping close to Ross and Christianson.

Ross scurried as best as he could with Kloet strung across his shoulders.

His bare feet were being torn to pieces from running over the gravel and crushed coral.

Christianson was right by Ross's side.

The flesh on the bottom of Christianson's feet was shredded and bleeding.

The old man was huffing and puffing and scrambling as fast as he could make his arthritic knees churn.

BAM!

BAM!

BAM!

BAM!

BAM!

Bullets were whizzing by their heads and zipping into the ground all around them as they valiantly continued their desperate flight to freedom.

Whap!

Ross felt something slap into his side.

Adrenaline had been surging through his body, and he wasn't exactly sure if he had been hit or not.

He tensed up and continued pushing himself forward with Kloet draped across his shoulders.

Move!

Move!

Move!

This was the only thought running through his mind.

But he could feel himself faltering.

Go!

Go!

Go!

Ross was stumbling now, but he continued pushing his body forward.

Come on!

Come on!

Come on!

Then Ross collapsed on the ground.

He hit hard and Kloet fell off his shoulders and splayed out on the ground like a rag doll.

Two of the bolder terrorists were less than ten meters behind them.

Ross rolled over and took aim with his Colt pistol.

He shot twice.

KA-POW!

KA-POW!

The nearest terrorist's face puffed up for half a second. At the same time the back of his head splattered apart, with blood and skull matter flying helter-skelter everywhere.

The next terrorist stopped dead in his tracks and collapsed to the ground with a forty-five ACP bullet hole to his chest.

Ross ran his hand down the right side of his ribcage.

He had been shot and blood was oozing from the wound.

It felt like one of his ribs was broken.

Christianson saw what was happening and threw his body over Kloet to shield him.

Kloet raised his head to see what was happening, but Christianson pushed it back down.

"Stay down!" he yelled.

Christianson aimed his Smith & Wesson revolver.

Another terrorist was advancing on their left.

Christianson shot once.

KA-POW!

The terrorist sunk to his knees and crumpled in a heap after Christianson's thirty-eight special bullet tore a hole through his neck.

In desperate situations, thinking and acting become one.

Professional soldiers react instinctively without hesitation.

Professional Secret Service Agents do the same.

Ross and Christianson knew what they had to do.

They were never going to leave Kloet.

They were Americans.

They were sticking together until the end.

Ross brought his knees up and then straightened his arms to push himself up from the ground.

He staggered to his feet and scrambled forward to where the two dead terrorists had fallen.

Ross snatched up their discarded AK-47 rifles and rushed back to Christianson.

"Here take this!"

Christianson grabbed the rifle and immediately aimed it behind Ross.

Two terrorists were trying to outflank his friend.

"Allahu Akbar!"

"Allahu Akbar!"

"Allahu Akbar!"

The terrorists were screaming and racing towards their position.

Christianson squeezed the trigger of the AK-47 and blasted off a burst of fully automatic fire.

The two terrorists fell dead with a dozen bullet holes stitched across their torsos.

Ross spun around and took a knee.

Three more terrorists were charging from the right side.

Ross pressed the trigger.

The AK-47 assault rifle bucked in his hands letting loose a fusillade of automatic gunfire that crumpled the terrorists in their tracks.

"Come on! Come on!" yelled Christianson.

Christianson bent over and grabbed Kloet. With all the strength he could muster, he pulled Kloet up and heaved him onto his shoulders in a fireman's carry.

Ross pushed himself to his feet.

Christianson reached out and grabbed Ross by his rumpled suit coat jacket.

"Come on Jimmy!"

Both men resumed their dauntless race to the life raft and freedom.

CHAPTER TWENTY-TWO

ALL IN

Back on the Albatross, Lin and Emanuel were watching as the scene unfolded.

They saw the searchlight turn on and sweep down, followed by bursts of automatic weapons fire lighting up the countryside.

Lin's hands went instinctively to her mouth. She frantically gasped in terror.

"We have to do something!" she pleaded to Emanuel.

"We have to help them!"

"We have to help them!"

Emanuel stared at Lin.

"What do you want to do, Lin?"

"We need to just get over there now!" she yelled.

"Where is your first-aid kit?" demanded Lin.

Emanuel scurried to the starboard side of the aircraft.

He pulled a white nylon bag emblazoned with a red cross off the wall and handed it to her.

"Here it is."

Lin grabbed the bag and slung it over her shoulder.

She hurried over to the trunk where Ross had been pulling out diving equipment, and grabbed a serrated-edged knife and sheath. She bent over and strapped the sheath to her right calf, making sure the knife was secure.

"Wait a second," said Emanuel.

He ran to the cockpit and emerged a few seconds later with two Chem Lights and a Heckler & Koch MP5 submachine gun.

He slung the MP5 over his shoulder and walked back to Lin.

Emanuel handed Lin one of the Chem Lights.

Lin stared at him.

"What?" he asked. "You'll need it."

He handed her a piece of parachute cord and said, "Hang it around your neck so you don't lose it in the water."

Lin threaded the parachute cord through a little lanyard loop at the tip of the Chem Light. Then she tied a square knot at the end and hung it around her neck.

Lin bent the tubular Chem Light, breaking the capsule inside and releasing the chemical mixture. Then she shook the light for a few seconds, back and forth.

The mixture ignited and emitted a yellow-green Halloweenish glow.

Lin said, "Do you have any more boats?"

"No," said Emanuel, igniting his own Chem Light.

"Okay, then we swim," said Lin.

She kicked off her sandals.

Without hesitation, Lin crouched in the open hatchway.

She curled her toes around the cold steel ledge and sucked in a deep breath of air.

Then she straightened her arms over her head and hurled her body out into the dark waters of the South China Sea.

Emanuel stuck his head out the hatch and said, "Swim for all you're worth, Miss Lin."

Kicking off his own tattered brown leather sandals, Emanuel bowed his head and jumped out following Lin.

Emanuel had landed his Grumman HU-16D Albatross seaplane about seventy meters from the coast. A seventy meter swim can be quite excruciating at night, with choppy seas, in a typhoon.

Lin was slicing through the waves expertly and making good time.

She used the crawl stroke and flutter kicked her legs.

She was determined to get to the beach and help out.

If this is the end, then I'll die with James and his friends.

I love him.

I will always love him.

Dear God if you exist help us!

Emanuel trudged through the sea with the MP5 submachine gun on his back.

He was an excellent swimmer, and with Lin's glowing Chem Light as a guide, was quickly by her side.

They swam, and swam, and swam.

The revolving lighthouse beam drew them in like gypsy moths to a light.

Lin was periodically raising her head up out of the water to scan the shore.

She could hear the sounds of the gunfight and see the muzzle flashes on the horizon.

Lin's petite white summer dress was creating drag against her body in the water as she swam.

This made her swim even harder.

The dress finally gave up the struggle and was torn free from her.

Now she streaked through the waters nude.

Soon Lin and Emanuel were both approaching the surf zone with the waves starting to break.

Emanuel was unexpectedly thrust up onto the beach by the swashing up-rush of water. He lay face down in the sand for a second and then struggled to his feet.

The water became foamy and bubbly, and now Lin's feet hit sand.

A seaweed bed was all around her, and Lin's body glided right through it.

The sticky, gooey seaweed enveloped Lin's naked body.

It wrapped around her and clung to her body like a slimy adhesive.

Seaweed was strung across her bosom and strapped across her back.

Seaweed caressed her thighs and became glued to her legs.

Her face and hair had greenish strands draped across like some Medusa mermaid from hell.

Lin could finally stand up now and moved through the surf zone to the beach.

The gunfight was raging on shore with bullets ripping into the sands and piercing the surface of the ocean.

Lin held her Chem Light up above her head in an attempt to see where Emanuel had landed.

A stray bullet struck the Chem Light and shattered it, spraying the glowing yellowish-green material all over Lin's nude body.

The chemical dripped down her face and across her back.

The glowing substance trickled down between her breasts and dribble over her legs to her feet.

CHAPTER TWENTY-THREE

SEA DEMON

Christianson had Kloet over his shoulders and Ross was at his side.

They were stumbling towards their moored life raft on the shore and their only means of getting Kloet back across the ocean to the seaplane.

The terrorists pursuing them were a combination of a few international hardcore Arabic speaking Al-Qaeda operatives, and mostly local homegrown Filipino Tagalog speaking Abu-Sayyaf and Jemaah Islamiyah. The local Filipino terrorists greatly outnumbered the outsiders.

BAM!

BAM!

BAM!

BAM!

BAM!

Bullets were tearing up the ground at Ross and Christianson's feet.

BAM!

A 7.62x39 millimeter bullet tore into Ross's right leg.

Ross faltered and was hobbling forward.

BAM!

BAM!

BAM!

Another bullet hit Ross in the right shoulder just above his clavicle.

Ross couldn't catch his breath and he collapsed to the ground.

Christianson turned and saw Ross fall.

"Keep going!" Ross yelled to Christianson.

"Keep going!"

Christianson stopped and dropped Kloet to the ground beside Ross.

The old Secret Serviceman flicked down his AK-47 selector lever switch to semi-auto to conserve his ammunition.

Four terrorists were charging their position from the right flank.

Bending down on one knee, Christianson took aim and fired his assault rifle.

BAM!

Christianson's bullet tore a hole through the first terrorist's stomach.

BAM!

The second terrorist spun around and collapsed to the ground with a bullet through his sternum.

BAM!

The third terrorist's head disappeared.

BAM!

The fourth terrorist received his full-metal-jacketed ticket to hell.

Ross sat up with his AK-47.

Two screaming terrorists were trying to rush Christianson.

Ross squeezed the trigger and shot the first man in his chest and the second in his open mouth.

Julius Creedmoor was running towards the firefight and thinking to himself.

This isn't even about Kloet!

This is about Ross.

Abu Sayyaf wants Captain James Ross dead.

There's a bounty on his head of two hundred and fifty thousand dollars American.

I'm going to deliver them Ross's head tonight.

And I'll give them Kloet as a bonus, he thought to himself.

Creedmoor was shocked by what he was witnessing on the ground.

He started to slow down and crept past corpse after corpse of his men.

Rage swept over Creedmoor, and he let out a string of profanities.

God damn it!

God damn it all to hell!

These "terrorists" can't even kill three men!

Back on the beach, Emanuel picked himself up out of the silt and spat sand out of his mouth.

He searched the shore with his eyes, left and then right, looking for Lin.

As he scanned the shore he saw something that he couldn't quite believe.

Across the sands there stood what appeared to be a glowing, illuminated, sparkling, heavenly angel.

He shook his head and stared harder, realizing what he was seeing was the glowing illuminated form of Lin Sparrow.

Emanuel ran over to Lin in utter bewilderment.

He pulled the Heckler & Koch MP5 submachine gun from around his shoulders and flicked off the safety lever.

Emanuel couldn't help but stare at Lin's yellowish-green, glowing, illuminated and lustrous, seaweed draped nude body.

"Are you okay Lin?"

"Yeah, come on!" yelled Lin.

Lin Sparrow pulled the serrated divers knife out of the sheath on her leg and began running inland up the beach.

Emanuel stayed right by her side, churning through the sand.

Lin followed the flashes of gunfire and saw where Ross, Christianson, and Kloet were making their final desperate stand.

Lin and Emanuel were coming closer and closer.

The terrorists were in disarray.

They had not expected such tenacious resistance from the American infidels. Some were beginning to wonder if Allah was really on their side.

Then they saw her.

First one, and then another terrorist saw the same thing.

They stopped in their tracks and motioned to one another to look.

They pointed their fingers and gasped in horror at the female apparition behind the three Americans.

"Ito ay ang satanas!" cried one terrorist in his native tongue of Tagalog. "It is the devil!"

"Dagat demonyo! Dagat demonyo!" yelled another terrorist saying, "Sea demon! Sea demon!"

Others stopped their assault on the Americans and pointed to the yellowish-green glowing seaweed draped beautiful woman who rose up out of the sea and was coming towards them now.

"Masamang bruha!" cried another terrorist proclaiming, "Evil witch!"

Still others knelt down and cried, *"Ito ay ang ina ng diyos!"* Roughly translated to mean, "It is the mother of God!"

The terrorist assault started to falter.

They thought Lin Sparrow was some kind of hellish sea-creature, or spirit from heaven. They weren't sure which.

Most were frozen with fear.

Several dropped their weapons and fell prostrate to the ground.

Creedmoor saw what was happening.

"Get up you idiots, get up!" Creedmoor yelled.

"God damned superstitious fools!"

"I'll show you."

Creedmoor looked to the ground and spotted a discarded assault rifle. He picked it up and methodically took aim at Ross, Christianson, and Kloet.

BAM!

BAM!

One of Creedmoor's bullets tore into Kloet's thigh.

Kloet let out a grunt of pain.

Christianson turned his head and saw Creedmoor advancing.

Swinging his AK-47 around, Christianson aimed and squeezed the trigger.

Nothing happened.

The weapon was empty!

He let the rifle fall out of his hands to the ground.

"Look out!" yelled Christianson desperately.

Before Ross or Kloet could do anything, Christianson threw his body spread eagled over them both.

BAM!

BAM!

BAM!

BAM!

BAM!

Creedmoor's bullets tore into Christianson's back. Bullets that were meant for Ross and Kloet.

Other terrorists saw what was happening and seemed to regain their composure. They picked up their weapons and started to regroup.

"Peter!" yelled Ross.

Ross shook Christianson, but there was no response.

Ross rolled Christianson off of him, and picked up a rifle.

He struggled to his feet and methodically took aim.

I'll go down taking as many of these sons of bitches as I can with me, thought Ross.

The sixteen terrorists still alive were slowly advancing towards Ross's position.

"Welcome to hell, bastards," he said through gritted teeth.

Ross started shooting.

The scene became a bloodbath of carnage.

Ross stood his ground and fired his assault rifle.

He fired, and fired.

But Ross was not firing alone.

Emanuel, with MP5 submachine gun in hand, ran up to Ross and now stood side-by-side with him.

Both men fired, and fired, and fired.

Ross emptied his AK-47. He threw it to the ground, and his eyes searched for another weapon.

He snatched one up and resumed firing.

Emanuel emptied his submachine gun as the three remaining Abu Sayyaf terrorists retreated and ran away.

Creedmoor let loose a wild, maniacal scream.

He leveled his AK-47 at Ross and Emanuel.

In his bloodlust, Creedmoor failed to notice Lin advancing on his blind side.

She was on top of Creedmoor now.

Lin drew her right arm back over her head, and plunged the serrated-edged knife deep into Creedmoor's back.

The rifle fell from Creedmoor's hands and clattered on the gravel at his feet.

A confused expression overtook his face.

Creedmoor moved his lips and tried to speak, but no words came out of his mouth.

He fell to his knees, and then collapsed face first onto the ground.

Lin rushed over to her friends.

She knelt down and pulled the first-aid bag from around her shoulders and tore it open.

Lin triaged the slaughterhouse in front of her.

She saw Ross and Emanuel standing, and thought they must be all right, so she attended to Kloet and Christianson.

Lin gently rolled Christianson over.

The old Secret Service Agent had been shot three times in the back by Creedmoor. He was gasping for breath and had blood gurgling out of his mouth.

Christianson was alive, but barely.

Lin sadly realized there was nothing she could do to save his life. It was only a matter of seconds.

She turned her attention to Kloet.

Kloet was shot clean through the left thigh and bleeding profusely.

Lin applied pressure to the exit wound with her left hand. With her right hand, she pulled out two surgical dressings from the first-aid kit.

Using her teeth, Lin ripped the sterile paper covering off of the dressings.

Then she pressed the dressings on Kloet's entrance and exit wounds, and wrapped surgical tape over them.

Lin grabbed Kloet by his chin and turned his head back and forth, but his body was still neuromuscular paralyzed. She saw the surgical tape on his black and blue forearm. Lin pulled the tape off and saw the puncture site where Kloet had been administered some drug intravenously.

"What drugs has he been given?" yelled Lin.

Ross thought for a moment about what he had read on the front of the intravenous bag.

"Um, vecuronium. Vecuronium bromide I think," said Ross.

Lin searched in Emanuel's first-aid kit.

She found an auto-injector of atropine.

Good old Emanuel, she thought.

The atropine auto-injector Emanuel had somehow gotten a hold of and stored in his first-aid kit was the dark green military type, commonly used as an antidote for nerve agent poisoning.

Emanuel had procured it from the old Navy Base at Subic Bay, where all his other equipment came from.

Lin learned in her nursing pharmacological studies that the drug atropine can also be used as an antidote for vecuronium bromide overdose.

She armed the injector by pulling it out of its plastic safety clip.

Lin firmly pressed the tip of the injector on Kloet's right thigh. The firm pressure automatically triggers the internal spring to inject the needle and release the antidote.

Lin held the injector on Kloet's thigh for ten seconds, and then pulled it straight away and dropped the mechanism to the ground.

Within seconds, Kloet started to come around.

Ross knelt down next to Christianson and cradled him in his arms.

"Peter. Peter, what can I do?" asked Ross.

Christianson's eyed fluttered open.

Blood was trickling out of the corner of his mouth, and he was gasping for breath.

Ross held Christianson's hand in his and squeezed it tight.

"Jimmy?" whispered Christianson.

"I'm here, Pete."

"Jimmy, did we win?" asked Christianson weakly.

Ross had tears in his eyes now.

"You bet we did, Pete," said Ross.

Christianson coughed up blood and smiled.

"Thank you Jim," said Christianson.

"For what?" asked Ross, with tears running down his cheeks.

"Thank you, for letting me help you," said Christianson.

Christianson let out his last breath.

He was dead.

Ross cradled Christianson in his arms and kissed him on the forehead.

"See you in the next life, Peter," whispered Ross.

Emanuel was standing next to Ross, and now knelt down beside him.

"Sir, let me carry Mister Christianson to the life raft. We need to get out of here sir, in case more come back," said Emanuel.

Ross nodded his head in agreement.

Emanuel reverently lifted Christianson's body.

Kloet was alert and sitting up now. Ross leaned over and helped him to his feet.

"Can you walk, Randy?" asked Ross.

"Yeah. Yeah I can. Whatever Lin gave me worked," said Kloet.

"Let's go," said Emanuel.

Lin looked at Ross's blood soaked clothes and gasped.

"James, you're wounded! You need help!"

Ross held up the palm of his hand to stop her.

"Later Lin. Let's just get out of here," said Ross.

Lin wrapped one of her arms around Ross's waist, and the other around Kloet's waist. Ross and Kloet put their arms around Lin's shoulders. She used her strength and body mass to support both men.

With Emanuel leading the way, they used the life raft to get to the Albatross and freedom.

The storm had finally broken.

The rain had disappeared to all but a very fine mist now.
The darkness of the night was over.
A new dawn was breaking.
The sun was spreading its warmth over the horizon.
And it looked like it would be a beautiful day.

EPILOGUE

Oh death, where is thy sting? Oh grave, where is thy victory?

1 Corinthians 15:55

TODAY

It was a beautiful day as far as Washington DC days go.

The early morning hours had felt the dark dreary effects of a sudden freeze, but now the eerie chill was leaving and the snow was floating down slowly and playfully over the National Capital Region.

The air had a crisp, solemn feel about it.

Ross looked at his watch.

It was a new Swiss Benrus Type I diver's watch that Lin Sparrow had given him. Lin had the watch outfitted with a custom stainless steel Olongapo bracelet engraved with his name and SF Team number.

It was just after eight o'clock in the morning.

Ross was wearing his blue Army Class A uniform under a long black Army issued trench coat.

He had recently been decorated with the Silver Star Medal for gallantry in action against the enemy. Along with the medal came a reassignment to the United States Army Operational Group, as the Chief of Operations Support Branch.

He purposely had arrived at the cemetery early, as soon as it opened.

Arlington National Cemetery affected Ross differently each time he visited.

He wasn't here today as a tourist.

He wasn't here today to look at history.

He was here to keep a promise.

A promise to a friend.

He walked purposefully with his head slightly bowed and hunched up his shoulders against the cold and snow.

He was looking for the sloping area below Arlington House, the former General Robert E. Lee home.

After about fifteen minutes, Ross was at his destination.

There was a long chain ringing the grave area suspended by three foot tall posts set at intervals to prevent tourists from getting too close.

The grave site reverently reflected the final resting place for four members of a family: two infant children, the First Lady, and the Boss.

The heavy snow had been swept off of the site early in the morning by the groundskeepers, and now there was just a light dusting of frost on the markers.

Ross stood and looked at the graves.

His breath was coming out in puffs circling and disappearing skyward as tears filled his eyes.

He reached into his black trench coat pocket and pulled out the five pointed gold star.

Carefully stepping over the chain with his right leg, he leaned forward and tenderly laid Special Agent Peter Christianson's U.S. Secret Service badge on the lower right corner of President John F. Kennedy's gravestone.

Ross pulled back and straightened up.

He looked down.

The eternal flame felt warm and invigorating against the cold.

He rubbed his hands together and smiled.

Turning around, Ross thrust his hands into the pockets of his trench coat and looked straight ahead.

He walked quietly away, and was soon lost to view in the mist of the gently swirling snow.

THE END

ABOUT THE AUTHOR

Bernard Cenney retired from the United States Army as a Lieutenant Colonel after more than twenty-eight years in uniform. He considers it a privilege to have served his country throughout numerous command and staff assignments the world over. He makes Texas his home.

www.ingramcontent.com/pod-product-compliance
Lightning Source LLC
Chambersburg PA
CBHW030420310726
48979CB00009B/1546/J

* 9 7 8 1 7 3 6 2 4 5 1 3 2 *